NOOR-UN-NISSA INAYAT KHAN

SUFIYA AHMED

D1350178

■SCHOLASTIC

For Rehan,

who loves tales of heroes.

First published in the UK by Scholastic Children's Books, 2020
Euston House, 24 Eversholt Street, London, NW1 1DB
A division of Scholastic Limited

London ~ New York ~ Toronto ~ Sydney ~ Auckland
Mexico City ~ New Delhi ~ Hong Kong

SCHOLASTIC and associated logos are trademarks and/or
registered trademarks of Scholastic Inc.

Text copyright © Sufiya Ahmed, 2020
Cover illustration by Euan Cook, 2020

ISBN 978 0702 30005 9

Printed and bound by CPI Group (UK) Ltd, Croydon, CR0 4YY
Papers used by Scholastic Children's Books are made from wood
grown in sustainable forests.

2 4 6 8 10 9 7 5 3 1

While this book is based on real characters and actual historical events,
some situations and people are fictional, created by the author.

www.scholastic.co.uk

Chapter 1

Abba

February 1927

It is February and the air is chilly with the season. The promise of warmth that comes with spring is still weeks away in our home city of Paris. On some mornings the ground is slippery with ice. As the eldest of the Khan children, aged thirteen, I am the one tasked with scraping it off our drive. We regularly have visitors and Amma doesn't want them to slip and fall on their way to the front door.

It is on one of these icy mornings that the sky caves in on my world.

I am bent over with a shovel, my favourite red scarf wrapped tightly around my nose and mouth, and my woolly hat pulled over my brows to keep my head and ears as warm as possible. With a deep breath I raise the shovel high above my head and bring it down hard on the ice. My hat slips over my eyes and I push it back impatiently to get a better view of the newly formed patterns. The thin cracks make interesting designs and I start to see stories in the shapes – is that a horse rearing up on its hind legs? A wolf pack running across the hills? Making up stories is my favourite thing to do, and my little brothers and sister are always desperate for me to tell them new and exciting tales. Abba says that one day, I might even be able to write books and make a living from my imagination. I hope he's right. It is my dream to become a children's writer when I grow up.

My latest story is about a girl who escapes the woods after becoming lost in them. Although initially scared, she finds the courage to face the darkness and danger and manages to find her way out. The moral of the story is that only the brave can find the light.

I'm very proud of it and I can't wait to read it to Abba. Of course, I'll have to wait until he returns home. Five months ago, he left to travel to his homeland, India, and he still hasn't returned. Amma, my siblings and I miss him so much and we're all hoping that he will come home soon. There is always more laughter, joy and stories to be shared when he is around.

"Hello, Miss Noor."

The voice startles me and I stumble back a few steps

before realizing it is only the postman. His black moustache is flecked with frost and his teeth chatter together.

He thrusts his arm forward and hands over an envelope. I glance down at it. Perhaps it is from Abba on his travels!

"Thank you, I'll take it to Amma now. Would you like to come in for a hot cup of cocoa?"

My offer brings a small smile to his face but he shakes his head, patting the sack over his shoulder. "Thank you, little one, but I have all this post to deliver."

He turns to walk away and I watch his feet. If he slips on the path, then I will know that I've missed a spot. To my relief, he disappears from view without stumbling. Satisfied, I turn my attention back to the ground. I need to finish scraping this last patch before I go indoors. A few minutes later, with the ice cleared, I turn to climb the steps to the big house at the top.

"Welcome to Fazal Manzil," Abba always tells visitors, with a big warm smile and open arms. "I have named our humble abode the 'House of Blessing' and you are all most welcome."

We came to Fazal Manzil five years ago. My father is the leader of a spiritual group and we moved around a lot so that he could share his teachings. I was born in Moscow, then we lived in London for several years before finally settling in Paris. But I know my father still has a special place in his heart for India. As a direct descendent of a king, a sultan whose family was exiled many years ago, Abba is loved by many people there despite the country being ruled by the British Empire.

Looking at Abba, no one would ever imagine him to be a royal prince. In my stories, princes wear bright, colourful clothes made out of silks and turbans decorated with jewels. They hunt tigers and lions whilst riding grand, majestic elephants. Not my abba. He dresses in simple robes and likes to write poems and listen to music. He is a peaceful man who believes in always telling the truth. He also calls himself a pacifist, which he taught me is someone who is against all violence and war. Abba is a big admirer of another famous pacifist, Mr Gandhi, who wants to free India from the British Empire.

Abba has many followers here in Europe, which is why our house is always open to visitors, and why I must scrape away the ice.

Halfway up the steps, my foot slips a little. Gosh! I must have missed a bit. I get to work again and soon the stone step is ice free. I straighten up and gaze out at the view. From where I stand, I can see the city of Paris spread out below. It is a beautiful view and I find myself looking forward to the summer, when I can spend my time reading books or dreaming up stories on these steps – losing myself in another world – without worrying about freezing to death.

The hallway of Fazal Manzil is warm and inviting from the logs burning in the fireplace. I shrug off my boots, coat, hat and scarf to go in search of Amma. I don't get very far as my feet trip over an object which nearly sends me flying head first. Luckily, I manage to catch myself just in time.

I pick up the long wooden string instrument, my *veena*, which I'd left in the hallway earlier. It is one of my most favourite things, a gift from Abba. I smile as I think about the new tune I've been practising, so that I can surprise him with it as a welcome home gift.

"Bravo, *Babuli*," he will say, applauding. "*Babuli*" is his pet name for me which means "Father's daughter". He very rarely calls me by my given name, Noor-un-Nissa.

I find Amma in her room at the top of the house. As I walk in, the small speck of the Eiffel Tower is clearly visible through the large bay window. Amma is sitting in an upright position on her red velvet chair, eyes closed in meditation. As there are no men in the house right now, she is not wearing her headscarf. Her light hair, so different from my own dark strands, cascades over her shoulders. I glance at the framed portrait on her nightstand and see a younger Amma with her arms around her parents. Back then, she was called Ora Ray Baker but then she met Abba and they fell in love.

Sometimes, I stare at the photo of my American grandparents, wondering what they are like and whether they are as jolly as they look in the photo. I can only wonder, as Amma chooses not to talk about them. They weren't very happy about her marrying outside their race and religion, and even went so far as to disown her. That's why my siblings and I have never met them.

I do wonder sometimes if they ever think about me and their other grandchildren. Even if they did, they've never once invited Amma back to their home in America, or written to be invited to France. Amma never looks sad about her parents though. She is always happy and laughing when Abba is around.

I know Amma has been missing Abba terribly these last few weeks and she has been meditating for longer and longer each day as a way of coping. I don't normally like to disturb Amma during her meditation – she looks so peaceful – but if the telegram is from Abba, she'll want to read it straight away.

"Amma," I say as softly as I can to ease her out of the meditative state.

Her lips curve into a smile as her eyes open, full of

warmth as always. "My darling, Noor, have you been outside in the cold long?"

"Not too long, Amma, I promise."

She takes the envelope and places it at her side without a glance, before taking my cold hands between hers to rub them warm. "You're such a good girl."

I nod at the envelope. "The postman delivered that letter while I was scraping the ice." I perch down on the armrest, my hands still clasped in hers. "It might be from Abba to tell us when he's coming home."

Amma releases my hands. "It's not from your abba," she says softly. "The handwriting is not his."

Trust Amma to recognize the writing without barely a glance! Disappointed that the letter isn't from Abba, I get to my feet as Amma's fingers fumble with the seal. I'm nearly out of the door when an anguished wail sends me running back into the room.

"Amma," I cry in alarm. "What is it?"

The letter falls to the floor as she crumbles into a ball. Frozen to the spot in horror, I glance from the discarded letter to Amma as she continues to howl.

Her cries are loud and mournful. Her face is buried in her hands and her body heaves with sobs. Bending down, I retrieve the paper to stare at the neat arrangement of words.

One sentence jumps out at me and my heart begins to thud.

... REGRET TO INFORM THAT HAZRAT INAYAT KHAN DIED ON 5th FEBRUARY ...

For a second the words blur and I have to blink a few times before I can re-read them. Even then, I can't believe it. The telegram claims that Inayat Khan has died. That is my abba. Abba cannot be dead! I drop to the floor, wrapping myself around Amma's shaking body, her cries vibrate through me and my own tears gather in my eyes as I try to make sense of what has happened. My wonderful, kind, peace-loving abba has died ... away from us – his family – who loved him the most. How could this have happened?

Our wailing brings the rest of the family to the room. My younger brothers, Hidayat and Vilayat, hesitate in the doorway looking scared. They look to me for an explanation.

"We've had some terrible news," I manage with a slight tremble in my voice.

My brothers continue to stare in their confusion. I take a deep breath and sit up straight. I know I must say the words out loud, but I am afraid of doing so. How can I utter the most awful news in the world?

"Noor?" Hidayat prompts.

I take another deep breath and then release the words. "Abba has died."

Their reaction is immediate and the tears flow. I remain on the bed as Amma and my brothers tightly embrace. My younger sister, Khair, pokes her head around the door.

"Why is everyone crying?" Big, frightened eyes gawk at the strange scene. Seeing my little sister looking so scared forces me to bury my own feelings of loss deep inside me. It dawns on me that as Abba is no longer with us, it falls on me to look after my family. Abba would want that from me as his eldest child.

Determined to do the right thing, I brush the tears off my face and sprint over to Khair, gathering her up in my arms.

"It's all right," I answer, hugging her tight. "Everything will be all right. I'm here to look after you."

I know I have to be strong for all of us, even though I want nothing more than to crumple into a heap like Amma.

Chapter 2

Royal Connections

May 1927

Three months later, we travel to India so that we can visit Abba's grave.

Amma, Vilayat, Hidayat, Khair and I make the journey on a ship. The sea voyage takes several weeks, time that I spend supervising my brothers and sister as they play on the deck. Even though I've taken on this role of responsibility, I try to make time for my writing, dreaming up stories of mischievous monkeys, brave lions and sly snakes in the Indian jungle. I share these adventurous tales with my brothers and sister every night before bedtime, where they sit and listen wide-eyed and captivated.

Throughout the journey, Amma spends a lot of her time resting in the cabin. I've overheard our concerned friends in Paris say that she will lose her frailty with time – once she comes to accept Abba's death. They say that perhaps sitting beside Abba's grave will help end her grief. I wish I could believe those words. I don't think Amma will ever get over Abba's death. It's as if a part of her has died with him.

*

India is everything that I imagined and more. Rich and poor. Old and modern. At times, I feel like I've been transported into the pages of a story set in the golden days of the emperor who built the Taj Mahal. At other times, the visibility of the English soldiers reminds me that India is now ruled by the British Empire.

The day after we arrive in Delhi, Amma walks with her arms linked through Vilayat and Hidayat on either side. I follow closely behind with Khair, her little hand tightly held in my own. We are slowly being led by one of Abba's followers to his resting place. When the man stops and bows his head, I know that we are finally with Abba.

Amma's slowly drops on her knees, her head buried in her hands as she weeps. I look at my brothers and sister and realize we are all crying. It seems being here by Abba's grave has finally released all the grief and emotion that I locked away on that cold February morning when we learnt of his death.

"Abba," I sob aloud. "We miss you so much. Your *babuli* misses you so much."

I gasp as a hand strokes my hair. Abba used to do that. I glance up and see that it is Amma who has reached out to comfort me.

We remain in Delhi for a few more days, visiting Abba every morning. With each passing night, my heart and head finally begin to accept that he is gone for ever.

*

The journey from Delhi to Baroda – where Abba's family home is located – is a long one as we're travelling from the north of the country to the west. The carriages have bars instead of windows and I feel soothed by the cold air blowing through my hair as the train speeds along. The vendors at every station sell us delicious snacks and our tummies are quite full by the time our train pulls into our destination.

Baroda is very different from Delhi. Over there, nobody paid us any attention, but in Baroda everybody stares at us when we walk outside. Complete strangers even smile and wave at us. My brothers just stare back, unsure how to react, but Khair happily waves back. I have no idea why they are giving us such attention and find myself wondering if it's because they can tell we've come from Europe. It can't be. All around us are English soldiers with the palest skin, and nobody pays them the slightest bit of attention.

One afternoon we are being driven in a horse carriage to the bazaar, the Indian market, so Amma can purchase some goods. As the carriage stops at a turning to give way to the approaching traffic, two old women sitting under a tree wave at us. Colourful bangles jingle on both arms as they do so.

"Amma," Vilayat says. "Why are those women waving at us?"

Amma manages a small smile. "It's because you are Tipu Sultan's family."

My ears perk up. I know all about Abba's famous ancestor, the sultan who was betrayed and died for his people. I make a vow to find out more about him while we are here in India.

The carriage is on the move again and I glance back over my shoulder at the friendly women, who are still waving at us. Khair, who seems to love all the attention, eagerly waves back. I raise my hand and do the same. People who don't even know us are pleased to see us – the least we can do is return the greeting.

Later that afternoon, Amma and my brothers and sister are having an afternoon nap. I close the bedroom door behind me and make my way to the living room downstairs as I don't want to sleep. The house which is normally so noisy with people is quiet. Everyone here is having a siesta.

I sit down at the small table intending to write a poem about Tipu Sultan but I realize I don't know much about him. Just at that moment there is a noise behind me and I turn to find one of the older maids has entered the room. Oh yes, I forgot that the servants don't sleep in the afternoon – they use this quiet time to dust and clean. Perhaps she could tell me about Tipu Sultan.

She catches sight of me and smiles in surprise – clearly she hadn't been expecting anyone to be awake either. I beckon her forward and she shuffles over to me, her ankle bracelets jingling with each step.

"I would like to write about Tipu Sultan." I point to the paper on the desk, "I don't know much about him. Please could you tell me?"

Her gaze widens. She looks positively horrified that I know so little of my most famous ancestor.

"Noor-ji, the great Tipu Sultan was your blood – he was your great-great-great-grandfather," she says, "and the rightful ruler of the Kingdom of Mysore."

"But why was he called the Tiger?"

"Because of his fierceness in battle and his strength," she

replies, suddenly becoming so enamoured that she punches the air with two fists. "He always said it is better to live for two days like a tiger than to live for two hundred years like sheep. His throne was supported by a carving of a tiger and his men wore tiger badges. Did you know that he killed a real tiger with his own hands?"

"Really?" I can't help wondering if that's true. I once saw a real tiger in the Paris zoo and its size was intimidating. Perhaps Tipu Sultan tackled a cub. I say as much.

"No! It was a full-size tiger!"

I nod quickly in case I have offended her, and then ask, "Is that why he was loved by everyone?"

She shakes her head and sighs as if the re-telling is painful. "Tipu Sultan fought like a tiger to save his people. Long ago, the men from Europe began arriving in ships to our land. They possessed weapons that we'd never seen before and soldiers ready to die for their cause. Slowly and painstakingly they began to conquer many places. From the north to the south, and from the west to the east, the kingdoms of the maharajas and sultans began to fall. They were either killed in battle or surrendered for their lives. Tipu Sultan never refused a battle. They say he did not do it for glory, but because he knew that the invaders would turn his people into slaves. It is not easy to defeat a tiger; he fought and won every time."

She lowers her eyes and voice. "Until he was betrayed by one of his own men who sided with the invaders. Tipu Sultan would have never lost if it was not for that act of treachery. He was killed in battle and his wife and children were thrown out of their own palace."

Betrayed by his own side. I cannot think of anything more shameful and cowardly on the part of the backstabbers.

Sudden sadness fills my heart at the thought of the violent end of my great-great-great-grandfather. He was killed in battle by the enemy, away from his family and loved ones. A death met in the battlefield with extreme pain. I wouldn't wish it on anyone.

The maid glances over her shoulder and then whispers, "Maybe you don't know this but Tipu Sultan's fight for freedom is still alive today. There are people who want the British to leave India. Do you know who Gandhi-ji is?"

Of course I know who Gandhi is. My abba was a big admirer of the man who wants to free India from the British Empire.

"Noor-ji," the maid says, "remember that you too have the blood of the Tiger running through your veins. Freedom is in your blood."

With those words, she picks up her duster and shuffles

out of the room.

I stare after her, wondering what to make of all this new information. Does she expect me to join the free India movement? Does she not realize I am only thirteen years old? Even if I did want to help the cause, Amma says that we will be leaving in a few days to return home to Paris. This trip has been good for me and my brothers and sister, helping us to accept that Abba is really gone and that we must learn to live without him.

Amma, on the other hand . . . well, we'll just take each day as it comes. I'm not sure that visiting Abba's grave has helped Amma deal with her grief. If anything, she looks even more depressed. Whatever happens though I know that I will look after my family – it's what Abba would have wanted from his *babuli*.

I'm also going to continue writing stories and then, one day, when I'm old enough, they can be published for the whole world to read.

Chapter 3

Leaving France

June 1940

"Noor! We need to leave," Vilayat calls impatiently from downstairs.

I turn to the red velvet chair and a sigh escapes me. Amma's jaw is thrust forward and her eyes downcast. This is her at her most stubborn.

"Come on, Amma," I say urgently. "It's time."

She raises her eyes, lips set in a straight line.

I move towards her. "We need to hurry up!"

"We can't just leave—"

I don't let her finish. "We are running out of time!"

Why can't Amma see the urgency in what we need to do? The day has finally arrived; the one that I've been praying would never come. And it's all because of that dangerous man, Adolf Hitler, the leader of Germany. They call him the *Führer* and he believes that the German race is superior to everyone else, and wants to expand Germany into other countries.

Last year on 1st September, Hitler invaded Poland. Two days later, Great Britain, France, New Zealand and Australia declared war on Germany. I remember the grim news being reported on the radio as I was having dinner with my family. The meal of rice and vegetables that I had prepared was left uneaten, our appetites vanished as we realized our country was at war. In order to help our side, Khair and I completed a training course in Nursing and First Aid with the French Red Cross.

It has been an anxious year with the radio always quick to report the Nazi expansion. In very little time, Hitler's army spread all over Europe, knocking each country's defence down and getting closer and closer to France.

Our nightmare came true on 4th June when most of France had fallen to the Germans. Our beloved country now finds itself at the mercy of the Nazis.

Today is 5th of June. Vilayat and I have decided to move to London and take Khair and Amma with us. My other brother, Hidayat, opted to join the French Resistance in the south of France. It is not too late for us to leave before Nazi soldiers roll into the city with their tanks, if only Amma would get a move on.

"Do you want Adolf Hitler to break the door down?" I struggle to hide my panic.

Amma's stubborn expression instantly changes to one of fear. Though it is highly unlikely that the German chancellor would be kicking down any doors himself – he has soldiers to do that dirty work for him – his name has that effect on many people. No one can quite believe that the man with the funny moustache is now the dictator waging war on half the world, unleashing violence and causing complete terror. There have even been reports in newspapers about people being rounded up and transported to prison camps. They say Jewish people, the disabled, the Roma people and those with different political opinions have been disappearing from cities and towns. No one is safe.

"But Fazal Manzil is our home," Amma whispers. "Your abba would never abandon it." Her voice catches, the lump in her throat preventing further words.

It has been years but Abba's death has permanently changed her. The laughter left her eyes that cold February day when she opened that telegram in this very room. Despite the time that has passed, she is still filled with grief. I know this house is tied to her memories of him, and that's why she hesitates to leave now, even in the face of a foreign occupying force.

I sit down on the edge of the bed to take her hand in mine. "I promise you we will return one day," I say gently, trying to keep the exasperation from my voice.

"When?"

I vowed the day we learned of Abba's death that I would look after my family. My brothers and sister have not been the only ones that have looked to me for reassurance since. Amma's question is impossible to answer, but I try anyway.

"We will return after that evil man has been defeated and has curled up into a ball of shame."

She shakes her head. "Men like that never feel shame."

"Noor!" Vilayat calls again.

Amma finally snaps out of it and gets to her feet.

Vilayat is standing at the bottom of the staircase. "At last!" he exclaims, running up the steps two at a time to meet her.

As he helps her down the stairs I run to my room to grab my most prized possessions. Taking central space on my mantelpiece is the copy of my first published children's book, *Twenty Jataka Tales*, which is full of stories of bravery and courage. Stuffing it unceremoniously into my bag, I open a drawer to retrieve the scroll for my university degree in child psychology. I look longingly at my *veena* in the corner of the room. I wish I could take it with me, but it would just be too heavy. *Besides*, I remind myself, *we'll be back*.

"*Noor!*" Vilayat has lost his patience. I take one last loving look around my room and then bolt down the stairs.

Amma allows him to guide her out of Fazal Manzil and into the front seat of the waiting car. My little sister, Khair, is already seated inside, eager to flee the coming danger.

"About time!" She jabs a finger at her watch. "I've been waiting for ages."

"Not now, Khair." I give her a pointed look as I climb in. It is not the time to tell Amma that she's been too slow to leave her home of twenty years. Khair purses her lips and sits back in her seat.

I'm just about to swing the door shut when I hear a voice calling my name.

I peer out of the window to see my closest school friend, Raymonde, hurrying towards the car. We have been in such a rush to leave that I hadn't even had a chance to go over to say goodbye. There is someone else with her and I realize it is another old school friend, Gilbert. I scramble back out of the car.

"I just need a minute!"

"Make it quick!" Vilayat yells from the driver's seat as I turn to embrace my friends who have now reached me.

"You're really leaving for London?" Raymonde says. She looks a little tearful.

"I've got to go," I say.

"Will we see you again?" Raymonde asks.

"We'll return," I promise. "This is our home. Are your family definitely not leaving?"

Raymonde shrugs. "Mama wants us to stay, so we are staying."

I nod. "Will you do me a favour and please keep an eye on the house?"

"Of course."

"Make sure you come back," Gilbert says.

I nod and, after one last hug, climb back into the car. I'm suddenly overcome with sadness and it is an effort to hold back tears. I don't turn my head to wave at them as we pull away – I don't want them to see me crying. I have to be brave moving forward.

"Do you think we are doing the right thing?" Amma suddenly asks.

Khair and I say nothing, leaving it to Vilayat to answer.

"Absolutely," he says firmly.

I gaze out of the window at the passing houses. I know all the people that live in them. Or, at least, I did. Like us, many of them have left now.

"Your abba wouldn't have wanted this," says Amma, jolting me out of my thoughts. "He didn't believe in violence."

"Amma," Vilayat says gently. "We have spoken about this already."

She has been against the reason behind this trip to London since the beginning.

She turns to me, searching for support. I lower my gaze and remain silent. I understand why Vilayat wants to go to England, because it's the same reason I want to go to England. They are refusing to surrender to Hitler and his soldiers, and we can help.

And then we can reclaim Fazal Manzil – our home. It holds memories of Abba and my childhood, and I want to do everything I can to fight for it.

I am leaving France today, but one day I will return with Amma, Vilayat and Khair, and be reunited with Hidayat. For that to happen, we need to defeat the Nazi regime.

"Amma," Vilayat begins firmly, "if an armed Nazi soldier came to your house and killed twenty people, wouldn't you be an accomplice to their deaths if you had the opportunity to kill the Nazi and didn't because of your belief in non-violence?"

Amma's mouth opens and then shuts again, at a loss for words.

"How can we always talk about doing the right thing and then not do anything to stop evil?" Vilayat demands, his fingers drumming on the steering wheel. "We can't just stand by and watch what the Nazis are doing. Even Abba wouldn't have wanted that."

It is clear to me that Vilayat has lost all patience now. I know he is determined to join the British Royal Air Force to fight the Nazis, and there is nothing anyone – not even Amma – can say to stop him. She seems to realize that too, as she sits in silence. I can guess from her rigid posture that she wants to say more but has decided there is no use in the face of Vilayat's determination.

I lean forward and squeeze her shoulder in an attempt to comfort her. I can't blame her for feeling she should uphold Abba's principle of non-violence. But I agree with Vilayat. Doing nothing in the face of the Nazi threat is wrong – I only have to look out of the car window at the empty Paris streets to know this. So many people have left, the shops are empty and the homes are bolted. People know that when the German troops march into the city, Parisian life will never be the same again. The Nazis will take over everything. More frighteningly, they will enforce their ideas of superiority about who is allowed to live freely and who is to be carted off to a prison camp.

I am certain we are doing the right thing. Adolf Hitler must be stopped.

Chapter 4

Battle of Britain

June 1940

I cannot describe the feeling of glimpsing land after hours spent on a cargo boat. Khair and I are standing by the railing, inhaling the fresh air. Amma and Vilayat are down below deck.

"I can see England." Khair points excitedly ahead. "We're here at last!"

The journey from France to England has been filled with anxiety. One question repeated itself in my mind: will we get there in one piece? Even as we sailed on the Channel, the Royal Air Force fighter planes soared above us, a stark reminder that we are in the middle of a war. There were grim faces all around at the frightening noise of the plane engines. Well, all except Vilayat. He could barely contain his excitement at the sight. It is so plain to see that he is itching to become a pilot. I secretly hope that I'll be able to do something useful to assist in the war effort too.

As we sail closer to land, more and more passengers come up on deck. The grim expressions are replaced with relief.

"Where exactly do we arrive again?" Khair asks.

"A town called Falmouth."

"Do you remember England much?"

I shake my head. Abba and Amma moved to France when I was a little girl and I have very few memories of my childhood in England. The only clear memory I do have is of a big square park outside our house where I played with Abba.

Khair dabs her hair with her handkerchief. It is slightly damp from the sea spray, as is mine. The excitement that was visible on her face only moments ago is replaced by a nervous expression. Her eyes are wide and she repeatedly licks her lips. She reminds me of the little girl who peeped her head around the door to see our amma wailing with grief. The day we learned of Abba's death.

Our bodies rock slightly with the lull of the waves. Reaching out, I grip the railing with one hand and place the other around Khair's shoulders. "Everything's going to be fine," I reassure her. "We've made it this far, haven't we?"

"I'm worried about where we go from here," she admits.

"Do you think the Mitchell family will be happy to have us as guests?"

I nod without hesitation. "Mr and Mrs Mitchell are followers of Abba's teachings and very good friends of our family. I am sure they will take us in."

Khair shifts her body closer to mine, much like when we were younger and she would snuggle up to me on the sofa or in bed to seek comfort. "I hope you're right, Noor."

It turns out that I am right. We are given a lovely, warm welcome by a very surprised Mr and Mrs Mitchell when we arrive at their house in Southampton, after a long bus journey from Falmouth.

"It's so good to see you again," Mr Mitchell beams at Amma. "How long has it been since we visited Fazal Manzil?"

Amma manages a small smile through her tiredness. "Too long."

"We can catch up later about old times," Mrs Mitchell fusses. "A quick meal and off to bed for you four. You all look like you're about to fall to the ground with fatigue."

Her words are like music to my ears. A bed and a pillow is all I need right now.

The next morning when we are all rested, Mrs Mitchell announces new plans for us over the breakfast table. "I am afraid to say that Southampton is not safe. The German Air Force, the *Luftwaffe*, fly their planes over us at night and drop bombs. Thankfully we had some respite last night or I'd be waking you all to get down to the shelters."

Vilayat leans forward in his chair. "How bad is it?"

"Bad enough," Mr Mitchell replies. "Many cities across the country are being targeted, it's not just Southampton. London is particularly bad, being the capital. Hitler thinks he can bomb us all into submission but he doesn't know the resolve of the Brits. We will continue to fight back under the leadership of Churchill."

Amma's spoon clatters in her bowl. I glance sideways to see her hands trembling. She lets go of the silver to clasp her hands on her lap, out of view.

"What does this all mean for us?" Her voice is timid and frightened. "We are not safe here?"

"It is safer to be inland," Mrs Mitchell admits. "We can help you move to Oxford or you can stay here with us."

"We will move," Amma says without hesitation.

"I want to join the RAF," Vilayat announces suddenly to Mr Mitchell. "How can I do that?"

"You'll have to go to London for that. I can take you." Mr Mitchell says, and when Vilayat nods eagerly, says, "Right, I'll accompany you to the capital so you can join the RAF and my lovely wife will travel with you ladies to Oxford to get you settled there."

*

I place the tray on the table before passing the teacups around to Amma and Mrs Mitchell in our rented room in Oxford. It is small with drab curtains and one sofa. We all sleep in the second room with its two double beds.

Khair is busy tuning the radio she has borrowed from the landlady.

"You need to be quicker than that if you're going to catch the speech," Mrs Mitchell says, taking a sip of her tea. "How hard can it be to find the BBC?"

"I'm trying. I'm trying." Khair's forehead is wrinkled with concentration.

Mrs Mitchell turns to me as I perch on the sofa's armrest next to Amma. We really could do with more furniture.

"Tell me about this fellow, Noor."

She is referring to General de Gaulle, the leader of the French Resistance whose speech we are waiting to hear on the radio.

"Well," I begin, "General de Gaulle refuses to accept the French surrender to the Nazis and is keeping the flame of resistance alive. Of course, it isn't safe for him to be in France so he has fled to England. I heard on the broadcast earlier that Mr Churchill has given special permission for the general to broadcast a speech."

"Yes!" Khair jumps up, grinning. She has finally managed to tune into the BBC.

The general's voice crackles through the radio – we've missed the beginning it seems.

"Make notes for Vilayat." Khair hands me paper and pen.

Our brother is in London with Mr Mitchell to join the RAF. Oh, how I envy him. I begin to make notes on the most inspiring and passionate parts of the speech.

Must hope disappear?
Is defeat final?
No!

For France is not alone!
She is not alone!
She is not alone!
She has a vast Empire behind her.

She can align with the British Empire that holds the sea
and continues the fight.

This war is not over as a result of the Battle of France.
This war is a world war.

I, General de Gaulle, currently in London, invite the officers
and the French soldiers who are located in British territory
to put themselves in contact with me.
Whatever happens, the flame of the French resistance must
not be extinguished.

By the end of the speech we are all quite emotional, including Mrs Mitchell.

"What fine words." She dabs the corner of her eye with a handkerchief. "Only a gifted leader can rally the troops."

"See, Amma," I say. "We have to fight back."

Amma squeezes my hand and nods. I smile at her through my tears. Finally, I think Amma has accepted the fact that those of us who are able will have to contribute to the war effort. It is not enough to sit on the sidelines whilst innocent people are murdered and countries invaded. If we want to live in peace, we have to be willing to fight for that peace.

July 1940

I empty the bloody bandages into the bin and make sure to secure the lid. It's mid-July and rubbish that is not disposed of properly only encourages rats. Being summer there is also no shortage of flies and insects.

I head back into the Fulmer Chase Maternity Home for Officers' Wives – the building has been converted into a military hospital providing treatment to injured soldiers. The Red Cross certificate that I gained in Paris means I can work as a nurse here. Amma is delighted that I've acquired this position. Personally, I'm not so sure how I feel about it as all I seem to do is do chores for the more senior nurses and doctors. Of course, every little helps during the war effort but all I seem to hear all day is: "take this" and "clean that".

After each long day, I'm somehow left with the feeling that I am still not of any real use to this war.

I open the door of the makeshift surgery room. It is empty except for a nurse. "Ah, there you are," she says over her shoulder. "If you could just clean up in here, please."

The door swings shut behind her before I can say anything. My shift is nearly over but cleaning the entire room means I will be staying back late. Oh well – the sooner I begin, the sooner I can go home. I roll up my sleeves to strip the sheets off the bed. It is obvious the last patient lost a lot of blood, and it has stained everywhere, including the floor. This'll take a while.

I think of Vilayat in London with the RAF and how lucky he is to be able to experience that. Later that evening, I voice my frustrations to Mrs Mitchell when Amma is out of earshot in the kitchen. "I feel like I'm being wasted there."

Mrs Mitchell sips tea. Like many of the English, she does seem to drink a lot of the stuff. "Well, what would you rather be doing?"

My feet are up on the sofa and I hug my knees to my chin. "I was walking home from the bus stop and there were two women in uniform riding motorbikes. It looked to me that they were delivering something to someone very important in the war's chain of command."

Mrs Mitchell nods wisely. "You want adventure, my girl."

She was absolutely right. "I do! I want…" I trail off as Amma and Khair enter the room. I don't want Amma to know how unhappy I am in my nursing role.

"This letter arrived from Vilayat," Amma says to me. "I thought we could read it together."

I nod and hold out my hand. Amma sits down beside Mrs

Mitchell whilst Khair sits on the single chair in the room. First the radio and now the chair. Khair has become very good at coaxing the landlady to hand over new items.

My eyes scan the letter, each word adding to the disappointment I feel for my brother.

"Noor?" Amma looks past Mrs Mitchell to stare at me. "Is everything all right?"

I lean over to hand the letter back to Amma. "Vilayat says that he has failed to qualify for the Air Force and has been instructed to join the navy instead."

Khair's reaction is immediate. "Oh no! Poor Vilayat had his heart set on becoming a pilot."

Amma reads the letter and then says, "He's trying to hide the disappointment in his words. My poor boy."

I forget about my unhappiness at my role and think of how my brother must be feeling to have his dream shattered this way. I'll have to convince him to see the bright side when I next speak to him. This war is about defeating Hitler and we must play whatever part we can. It should not be about personal ambitions, but about the bigger picture of saving Europe from a tyrant. I'm sure the navy will play just as important a role as the RAF.

August 1940

Now that Vilayat is enrolled in the navy, Mr Mitchell has made his way back to Southampton and so Mrs Mitchell will be leaving soon. But first, she has some business to attend to in London before she heads back to be with him, and has invited me along.

I am so excited! I have been holed up between our accommodation and the hospital since we arrived, and I'm desperate for a change of scenery. Amma is not very happy about the outing – she doesn't think London is safe, with all the bombings.

"It's only for a day," I reason. "We'll be back before nightfall."

Amma's lips are set in a straight line. I know she still disapproves but I'm going anyway. I suppose I have inherited her stubborn streak.

We catch an early train and arrive in the capital by mid-morning. London is a shocking sight. There are crumbling buildings that are standing in their half-blown state with heaped rubble still to be cleared. At one point, we pass a crater in the ground where a bomb has dropped. It's just a giant hole which everybody skirts around. A few metres down, a bus is half buried in rubble. I wonder if it had any passengers when it rolled into the earth. I hope not. Glancing around, I wonder what Abba would have made of all this – no doubt the violence would have saddened him greatly.

"Don't touch the walls, dear," Mrs Mitchell says as we make our way to the restaurant in Russell Square to meet her friend. "One nudge and those bricks could come tumbling down."

I am careful to keep my distance from the crumbling buildings as we carry on walking. We're almost at Russell Square when a strange wail starts up, making us jump out of our skins. It's unbearably loud and everyone around us springs into action. Though I've never heard it before, I know the noise is an air-raid siren, blasting out from speakers all over the city. It's a warning that the *Luftwaffe* are above us in the sky, getting ready to drop bombs.

Mrs Mitchell grabs my hand in a panic. "What do we do?" she cries.

"Let's follow the crowd," I reply, frantically looking around at the people spilling out on to the street. "Everybody must be heading to a shelter."

We fall into line with a group of young women. One of the girls catches my eye and smiles. Perhaps she has noticed that Mrs Mitchell and I are not Londoners. It is amazing how calm they all seem – as if this sort of thing happens every day. Perhaps Amma was right; maybe it wasn't such a good idea to visit London during such uncertain times.

"Where are we headed?" I ask the girl who smiled at me.

"To Russell Square Underground station," she replies. "I don't think we are supposed to be using the Underground for shelter but it's the closest place where we'll be safe. We just have to go down to the platforms."

The stairs leading down to safety are long. I have never used the Underground and had no idea the tunnels are built so deep below the surface. Halfway down the steps Mrs Mitchell stumbles, but she is held upright by the crowd of people surrounding us.

"Are you all right?"

She manages a brave smile. "Just a bit clumsy, dear."

We reach the platform and settle down on the ground like everybody else. Hundreds of people are huddled together, and I imagine from the way they have set out blankets and are sharing food with each other that they expect to be here for a while. Some are talking in groups, whilst others are silent as we listen for sounds overhead.

We remain on the platform for hours. Mrs Mitchell and I don't talk much, preferring to listen to those around us.

"My husband thinks it is a good thing Churchill is in

charge," someone says.

"My mum says the same thing," adds the girl who told us to follow her in here. "She says he'll win the war for us."

Heads nod all around.

It is early evening when we finally emerge out of the station. I look around and don't see any signs of the attack.

"It was a false alarm."

I turn in the direction of the woman talking to another. False alarm? That's a relief! I step closer so I can catch more of her words.

"They keep warning us that the *Luftwaffe* will try to breach our air defences to bomb us in the daytime," the woman continues. "They haven't managed it yet, thanks to our Air Force boys."

The other woman shakes her head gravely. "It's only a matter of time before they do."

I close my eyes briefly. Another day where I have been saved from real danger. It's always been in the distance; the Nazis at France's borders, their troops marching into Paris after we left. Southampton was under the threat of bombing, but we weren't there long before we moved to Oxford, which is less of a target. The danger has always been in the background, being talked about and reported. I realize that I haven't experienced real fear – until now, hiding in an underground shelter where I believed bombs were being dropped overhead.

I look around at the Londoners on the street and all I can feel is admiration for their spirit. They appear so resilient as they go about their business. I want to be like them – fearless in danger.

"Noor, dear, I think we should return to Oxford."

I nod just as an ambulance and fire engine speed past. The drivers and attendants are all women.

"Let's catch a bus back to Paddington station," Mrs Mitchell says, leading the way to a bus stop across the road. "False alarm or not, to be in the middle of it was just too much for my nerves and…"

Mrs Mitchell is chatting away but I'm not really listening. My mind is occupied with a poster on the side of a bus. It's a glorious image of three young women posing next to a fighter plane. They are dressed in the blue uniform of the Royal Air Force and they look so happy and confident that they are positively glowing.

SERVE IN THE WAAF WITH THE MEN WHO FLY

Gosh, that sounds so incredibly wonderful and important. I decide right then and there to find out more. The RAF plays a vital role in both the defence and offence in the war. That's why Vilayat had his heart set on becoming a pilot. Sadly, his dream was dashed, but perhaps I could play a part by aiding the men who fly fighter planes.

We came to England to aid the war effort. Maybe this is the job I am meant to do. I want to be like those women on the poster in their blue uniforms – powerful and focused.

Chapter 5

Becoming Nora

October 1940

I close the front door and head for the kitchen with my shopping bag, which contains only a loaf of bread and a bit of cheese. Because of the war, Britain can't import food from other countries, so supplies are limited. We have little ration books, and are only allowed a certain amount of essential foods like milk, butter and cheese. When we first received our ration book, I was pleased to see that vegetables and fruit were not included in the coupons.

The government has been encouraging us to eat more potatoes. They are home grown so there are plenty to go around, but I still prefer bread. We have been in England for four months now and I still can't get used to the food here. I would do anything for a French baguette right now! Still, this bread is better than nothing and I try to feel more cheerful as I slice it, then divide up the cheese.

"Is that you, Noor?"

"Yes, Amma," I reply, suddenly feeling nervous about telling her of my new plans.

After returning from London with Mrs Mitchell, I made enquiries about the WAAF. It stands for Women's Auxiliary Air Force and they have an office in central Oxford. Setting off early, I walked to the address given to me by a senior nurse at work so that I could make an application to join.

I cannot describe the excitement I felt when I wrote down my details. Finally, I'd be able to do something *really* useful for the war. The image of the women on the posters keeps flashing before my eyes.

I think I understand now why Vilayat had his heart set on becoming a pilot. He is now enrolled in the navy and, from his letters, it is quite clear that it is hard work. Even after he didn't get his dream job, he still works hard to contribute to the war effort in any way he can. He understands that this is bigger than us.

I finish preparing a few sandwiches and put Khair's share aside for when she returns from her shift. She has recently joined me at Fulmer Chase hospital, but unlike me, she actually enjoys the work and is thriving.

Picking up the tray I join Amma, who is seated by the window in the living room staring out at the empty street. I think she feels a little lonely now that Mrs Mitchell has returned to Southampton. We all do. She was our only real friend here and I don't think we realized how much she did in terms of getting us settled until she left.

Amma takes her plate but doesn't eat. I dig into my sandwich, suddenly feeling famished. I'll most likely need the energy for when I inform her of my plans.

Swallowing the last bite, I try to find the words.

"I have applied to join the WAAF," I say, simply.

Amma turns her head and I see the alarm in her eyes. "What will it involve?"

"Well, with all the men off doing the fighting, there's a shortage of people operating the telephones, plotting the aeroplane routes and that sort of thing. I suppose I'll be doing something along those lines."

"But why do you have to join it?"

"Because I want to. It's an important role," I insist, and then add what I hope will make a difference. "The Queen is Commandant in Chief of the WAAF."

It fails to impress. "You are a nurse. You are already helping the war effort here and don't need to go gallivanting off doing something dangerous!"

"Amma!"

"I've already lost your abba," she says in a desperate voice. "Your brother has enrolled in the navy and now you."

"But—"

"I don't want you anywhere near the fighting."

"I won't be! Honestly, why do you think I will end up in the middle of a battle? I'll be based right here in England, not flying over enemy territories. And it's important work." She seems to pause in thought and this encourages me to continue. "Remember what we agreed when we left Paris? That we will do whatever we can to defeat Hitler and his Nazis in Europe. You remember General de Gaulle's speech when we arrived."

I am met with silence and Amma returns to looking out of the window, which only means one thing – discussion over.

*

A few days later, it seems Amma is going to get her way when an official-looking note addressed to me drops through our letterbox. My nervous excitement turns to disappointment as I scan its contents. My WAAF application has been rejected? And for such silly reasons!

I rush upstairs, pull out a piece of paper and sit down on the sofa to write.

My pen hovers over the paper as I try to articulate my feelings.

Dear sir,

I am writing to you to express my dismay and disappointment at being rejected from joining the WAAF.

The tears blur my eyes and I brush them away angrily. How dare they reject me? Every person counts – don't they? That's what all the posters pasted on buses and boards say. The WAAF's reason is just so pathetic – so what if I was born in Moscow? I am the daughter of an Indian man and have a passport that reads "British Protected Person". I am part of the British Empire through my Indian heritage. How can I be prevented from defending Britain just because of where I was born?

A few days ago, I read a newspaper article that said millions of people from across the British Empire are joining Churchill's war. It said that around two million people have signed up from South Asia alone. This little island cannot win against the Nazis on its own. Hitler can only be defeated by the full might of the British Empire. I shall give the people in charge at the WAAF a piece of my mind.

It isn't long before another note arrives. I gasp as my eyes race over the words and hug the letter tightly to my chest, ready to burst with happiness. Rushing into the sitting room where Amma is having a cup of tea, I try to compose myself. I know my news will not be met with delight, but it's hard to hide my excitement.

The sun streams in through the window, casting shadows on Amma's tired face. She sits hunched over, staring into her steaming mug of tea as if it holds the answers to all her problems. I take a deep breath.

"I've got some news, Amma," I begin. "The WAAF have sent a reply to my complaint. They've apologized."

Amma gives me a small smile, but her gaze flickers anxiously across my face. She knows there's something I'm not telling her.

"They've also sent me an appointment letter," I carry on hurriedly. "They want me to join them."

Amma manages to keep the smile on her face, but I can tell it is taking a lot of effort. I know her feelings haven't changed since we last spoke about the WAAF, but she is trying to be brave for me.

November 1940

"Name?" The woman behind the desk snaps impatiently.

I have decided to call myself Nora instead of Noor, as I imagine it will be easier for people to remember. It sort of feels like a new identity, or an alter ego of some sort. Vilayat had written in one of his letters that the other men at the RAF struggled to say his name, so in the end they just registered him as Vic.

"Nora what?" The woman logging my details at the WAAF office doesn't look up.

"Inayat Khan."

"What?"

I hesitate. Vilayat was right – people here really do struggle with different sounding names.

"Baker," I say, giving my mother's maiden name instead.

"Religion?"

"Church of England." Even though I come from generations of Muslims, it might be easier to blend in if I state the main religion of England instead.

"And what is your occupation?"

"I've been working as a nurse at the Fulmer Chase Maternity Home for Officers' Wives for a few months.

Before the war, I was a writer." I say it proudly, thinking of my published book of children's stories. I hope that, once all the fighting is over, I might be able to write another – maybe about my adventures in the war!

"Expertise?"

I draw a blank. I wasn't expecting that question! What am I good at, apart from writing children's stories?

"Erm ... I don't know."

The woman looks up at me for the first time. She takes in my appearance, no doubt noticing my darker skin and hair. "Well, let's see. Do you speak any other languages?"

I nod. "Yes! I speak fluent French."

Her green eyes widen a little. "Where did you learn to speak fluent French?" she asks.

"I grew up in Paris," I reply. "I went to school and university there."

Slowly, the woman raises her pen to her mouth and chews on the end as she takes me in. I can't help but feel she is looking at me in a new light. Finally, she removes the pen from her mouth and scribbles on the form.

"Fluent French. Good. We'll be in touch."

Chapter 6

Dots and Dashes

November 1940

A few weeks later, I find myself checking into a hotel in Harrogate, Yorkshire. I feel quite nervous as I stand under the twinkling chandeliers, my little suitcase clutched tightly in my hand.

The WAAF has selected me to train as a wireless operator with forty other women, and this is where I will be spending the night before training starts tomorrow morning. A few other recruits are staying at the hotel too and we spend the evening getting to know each other.

I try to enjoy myself, but my mind keeps slipping back to our rooms in Oxford where Amma and Khair are probably sitting together, worrying about me and my brothers. Saying goodbye this morning was difficult, but I know I'm doing the right thing. It takes me a long time to get to sleep that night, despite the comfortable bed.

The next morning, I feel a whole lot better as I gaze at my reflection in the mirror. My lips curve into a small smile. I'm wearing my very own shiny, blue uniform, just like those women on the WAAF promotion posters. I cannot shift the feeling of excitement that surges through me. Finally, I am going to be able to contribute to the war effort.

I do a quick twirl then grab my bag and run out of the door. All the girls are meeting downstairs for breakfast before we make our way to Ashville College, where we will remain for the first part of our training. From what I've heard, there will be lessons on radio communication and physical exercises. I can't wait to get started!

*

As the rain slashes at my face and the wind stings my eyes, I realize I underestimated how brutal the physical exercises would be. I am out running cross country with the other trainees, and after a few days at Ashville, I can safely say that this is the part of the day I hate the most. I was never very good at sport in school and I've quickly realized that I'm not any better now. Yet, here I am pushing myself through rain, wind and mud.

"Come on, Nora!" One of the other girls shouts over her shoulder. "You're falling behind."

I will myself to run faster but my legs don't obey.

Other than the physical part of my training, which I really don't enjoy, I'm happy to be here. I feel a sense of independence and freedom, which is something I never felt growing up at Fazal Manzil, with all the responsibilities on my shoulders.

I wear the same uniform as the other women, and eat and sleep beside them. Here, nobody knows me as a member of a royal house. Here, I am simply Nora Baker. And it is that simplicity that I love. Of course, that doesn't mean it's easy. There are drills and inspections, and it is rather cold and muddy, but it's wonderful to be part of something away from my family for the first time. Here, I'm part of something bigger than myself.

December 1940

My training at Harrogate ends a month later and, having been chosen to specialize in wireless telegraphs, I'm transferred to Edinburgh. I'm told that the course will last six months. To my delight, Amma and Khair decide to join me in Edinburgh, and rent a flat near my dormitory so I get to see them quite frequently.

My training involves learning how to communicate with a secret language called "Morse code". From the very start, I realize that it is going to be incredibly hard, but I'm determined to master it.

"Morse code," the instructor booms at the front of our first class, "was invented by Samuel Morse in the early 1800s. It is a form of communication which works by keying in a series of electronic pulses. A short pulse is a dot and a long pulse is a dash ..."

By the end of the lesson, I am excited to get started and try out this new secret language for myself. That evening I pore over my signs sheet. I must learn the symbols for each letter and number in order to code and decode messages.

A is ·—
B is —···
C is —·—·
D is —··
E is ·
F is ··—·

G is ——·

H is ····

I is ··

J is ·———

K is —·—

L is ·—··

M is ——

N is —·

O is ———

P is ·——·

Q is ——·—

R is ·—·

S is ···

T is —

U is ··—

V is ···—

W is ·——

X is —··—

Y is —·——

Z is ——··

1 is ·————

2 is ··———

3 is ···——

4 is ····—

5 is ·····
6 is —····
7 is ——···
8 is ———··
9 is ————·
0 is —————

I begin with my own name.

N —·
O ———
O ———
R —·—

It is like being five years old again and learning the alphabet for the first time. Except I don't remember that being as difficult as this! I sit back with a sigh.

*

"Hey, Bang Away Lulu, fancy joining us for lunch?"

I look up at the group of girls walking past my table and smile. Some of the other wireless operator trainees have nicknamed me "Bang Away Lulu" because of the heavy-handed way I type Morse code. I don't mind – we have nicknames for the other girls, too. It keeps our spirits up as we struggle through the Edinburgh winter. It's so cold here that I suffer from chilblains. My fingers and feet have swollen up and they itch all the time. Sometimes at night the pain gets so bad that I can't sleep.

One of the girls leans in to give my hands a friendly rub. "Get your blood circulating, Nora."

I laugh and jump off my stool to join them for lunch, but immediately regret it. The hard leather of the WAAF uniform shoes digs into the skin around my ankles. That's one more cut and blister added to my poor, shredded feet. How long is it going to take me to break them in?

April 1941

My time in Edinburgh is over by April, and two months later, I receive my first posting as Aircraftswoman First class to HQ No 6, RAF Bomber Command at Abingdon in Oxfordshire.

I am happy to be going back down south to Oxfordshire, which is at least a little warmer than Edinburgh. Khair is now studying medicine at a university in Edinburgh and will remain there while Amma returns with me and finds herself a new job in a hospital.

I try not to feel anxious about her, but she's getting so frail that I'm worried she will find the work too strenuous. Each time I see her, she looks a little thinner, a little more drawn – just a shadow of the cheerful woman I knew all those years ago in Paris, before Abba had died. I try to talk to her about it, suggesting that she cuts down on her hours of work, but she just nods and smiles then ignores all my advice. I suppose we are not so different!

I make sure to visit her on my days off. Abingdon is not far from Oxford and I usually cycle to save the bus fare. My new friend, Joan Clifton, sometimes joins me. We met on my first day at Bomber Command and hit it off straight away. She is lots of fun. We share a room at our WAAF accommodation and we both love music. We've even rented a radio together so we can sing along and dance in our room.

Joan and I transmit and receive messages side by side every day using Morse code. I'm so pleased to be contributing to the war effort. Hopefully, it's just a matter of time now before we finally defeat Hitler.

July 1942

A year has passed, and Joan and I are still in Abingdon with Bomber Command. We have been doing the same work for months and months, and although necessary to the war effort, we both feel the urge to try something new. With this in mind, Joan and I apply for new commissions. She receives hers in no time, whereas I am ordered on to a seven-week training course in Wiltshire. I'm annoyed that I haven't been given a new role, like Joan, but at least it will be a change of scenery!

"I'll miss you," Joan says trying to squeeze her sweater in the over-packed suitcase on her bed.

"Wiltshire isn't too far." I sit down on the case so that Joan can shut it. "We'll make the effort to meet up."

"What's the new course about?"

"Signals and instructions." I glance down at the case beneath me. "Is it shut?"

Joan nods and we both straighten up. "It's a little odd, don't you think?"

"What?" I ask.

She gives me a funny look. "It's like they're training you for something specific."

I shrug. I hadn't thought of it like that.

*

I quickly settle into the training programme in Wiltshire. It involves a lot of maths, geometry and trigonometry, which it turns out I'm pretty good at. In fact, I'm even better than a lot of the men. This makes me feel proud and boosts my confidence in my own abilities. I'm sure my achievements are being noted by superiors. Hopefully, I am now closer to a new commission.

August 1942

Vilayat has been granted a few days leave and is visiting Amma. With my training over, I've been sent back to Bomber Command in Abingdon and am working the same old shifts again. On my day off, I cycle over to Oxford to see them both.

Amma is preparing a meal for us in the kitchen and Vilayat and I are sitting together on the sofa. He says very little about navy work and I get the impression that he would rather talk about something else. I mention the letter that I received a few days ago finally calling me for a new commission.

"That's wonderful news," he says, beaming at me. "The change will be good for you."

I nod happily. "Yes, I can't wait."

"Have you thought about the questions they might ask about Indian Independence?"

The smile falls from my face. "What?"

"You know, the movement to free India from the British Empire?" Vilayat says, looking closely at me.

I make a face at him. Of course I know about that. Abba was an admirer of Gandhi, the leader of the movement. Suddenly, I feel very nervous. "Do you think they will bring it up?"

"You're the daughter of an Indian man," Vilayat says. "So, yes, I think they will. The struggle of the Indian people to free India from the Empire is no secret. I've made some Indian friends in London and it's all we can talk about. Gandhi's a small, elderly man, but he's given so many people strength. Did you know the British have locked him up in a prison now? Churchill hates Gandhi and his cause. He wants to make sure the crown jewel of the Empire does not break away under his watch."

I bite my lip, my mind whirring about how I would even begin to answer a question on India in the interview.

Vilayat pats my arm, taking pity on me. "You'll be fine, Noor," he says. "Anyway, tell me why you wrote to me for money?"

I shrug. "I only wanted a loan. It was just a small amount to pay for a new hairstyle. Everyone's got the new Eugene perm, you know, the wavy curly hair? I'd like that too but I'm a little short of cash."

Vilayat digs into his pocket and hands me an amount. "Go get it done, Noor. You deserve it. You've taken such grand care of us always."

*

The day of the interview finally arrives. My hair is fashionably styled and my tummy full of nerves as I sit across a table from four middle-aged men in a government room.

The first few questions are straightforward and then ...

"Miss Khan, we understand that your father was from India. Is that correct?"'

"Yes," I reply to the four men sitting on the other side of the table. There is a long pause and I shift in my chair – I know what's coming.

"How do you feel about Indian independence from the British Empire?"

There it is. The question that I have been dreading for days is delivered with direct simplicity. Of course, I knew the subject would come up. How could it not?

I am a big admirer of Churchill's passion to defeat the darkness brought upon us by Hitler. However, after my conversation with Vilayat, I've decided that when the war is over I shall become more active in the struggle for Indian independence.

People and nations should be free. Isn't that why we are fighting the Nazis? Because we want to be free of occupation. In that same spirit, I believe that India should be free. Abba taught me that I should never lie and I do not.

"I believe that the Indian people should be given their freedom."

A pin drop could be heard in the silence that follows. I clear my throat and attempt to explain my position.

"However, I also believe that the Indians should not press for independence at the moment. Instead, I think we should all focus on defeating Hitler. Indian independence can come after the war."

The men stare at me, aghast.

I swallow slowly. I have no doubt I have shocked them with my support for Indian independence and talked myself out of a new commission.

"Thank you, Miss Khan." The words are delivered stiffly by one of the men.

I am dismissed. I scrape my chair back and rise to my feet. My heart is racing. How can I rectify this? Where do I even begin? But I know that I cannot lie. I believe that after this war ends, India should be free.

My great-great-great-grandfather, Tipu Sultan, had fought for his country's freedom. He was betrayed. He had lost. Nearly three hundred years later, this new generation of Indians deserve to win. India's people deserve their freedom.

I close the door behind me, accepting that I won't be receiving a new commission any time soon.

Chapter 7

Becoming Churchill's Spy

October 1942

I gulp down the tea. It's lukewarm and weak, and feels more like I'm drinking dirty dishwater than tea.

The ten-minute tea break at work doesn't allow enough time for me to brew my own so I have no choice but to grab one of the cups already made in the canteen. As I finish the last drop, I remember the letter that I'd stuffed into my bag this morning as I'd left for work. I've had no time to read it because we've been so busy with the operating boards this morning. It looks too official to be from Khair up in Edinburgh, or even Vilayat. Thankfully, he passed his navy exams in September and is now a naval officer on HMS *Collingwood*.

I burrow into my bag to retrieve the letter. Hairpins jab my fingers before I feel the smooth paper envelope. Pulling it out, I strip the seal and begin to read. My mouth falls open as I absorb the words.

The letter is from the War Commission office inviting me to an interview at 1600 hours on 10th November to Room 238 at Hotel Victoria, Northumberland Avenue, London.

Finally! I am finally being called up for a new commission. My opinion on Indian independence had not disqualified me from gaining a new position.

"All right there, Nora?" One of the pilots grins as he collects a cup of dishwater tea from the tray.

"Yes," I beam.

He takes a swig from his cup and pulls a face. "Awful stuff, this."

"Oh, it's wonderful," I gush to myself, referring to my letter.

He gives me a funny look, thinking I'm talking about the tea. "If you say so."

November 1942

The hotel in Victoria I have been summoned to is neither elegant nor posh. In fact, it is rather scruffy. I climb the stairs to the third floor and wonder what the War Office is doing conducting interviews in a place like this.

I am ushered into a dull-looking room with a single desk, some chairs and little else. At the far end, the long, heavy curtains are partly drawn and I wonder if it is to keep prying eyes out. There is something extremely unusual about the whole set up.

A man comes in after me. He is tall and slim, and dressed in a brown suit. "Hello, Miss Khan."

I want to sound strong and authoritative but when I reply to his greeting, the voice that emerges is no more than a squeak. He strides over to me and to shake my hand – his grip is firm.

"Thank you for coming."

I nod and allow him to lead me to one of the chairs. His own seat on the other side of the desk looks no more comfortable than mine. In fact, it looks crooked, as if one of the legs is shorter than the rest.

"My name is Selwyn Jepson," he says, "and I am a recruitment officer."

"For the War Office?"

A short pause, then, "No, Miss Khan, this is not the War Office. That would be in Whitehall."

My heart gives a little flutter. Who is this man and what is this place?

"We have been watching you since your recruitment to the WAAF and…" His voice trails off as he shuffles through some papers in the file in front of him. "I see that your Morse code training earned you full marks. Well done."

I don't know what to say. I had no idea anybody had been watching me, and can't think why they would have been. For a horrible moment, I wonder if I am in trouble for supporting Indian independence.

"You are probably wondering why you are here." He leans forward and smiles for the first time. "May I call you by your first name?"

I nod. "It's Nora."

His smile broadens. "I know."

Of course he does.

"The Prime Minister has tasked me to recruit people who possess special skills. They could have exceptional operator skills, or knowledge of foreign languages, or even a daring attitude to life. This is the reason you are here."

"Oh." My mouth falls open and I hastily close it. The free world is looking at Mr Churchill to lead them to victory and that same leader has a job for *me*? I feel a tingle of excitement.

"Tell me, Nora. What do you know about the SOE?"

I rack my brains, but I'm pretty sure I've never heard of it before.

"The Special Operations Executive," he clarifies.

I curse inwardly. I should have prepared for this meeting better. I'm totally oblivious to what Mr Jepson is talking about and I can't pretend I know about something I don't.

"I have never heard of it," I admit.

"That is good."

"Oh?" I reply, puzzled. This meeting is confusing me already!

"It is a secret organization."

"Ah." It seems it was a good thing I did not pretend to know about it.

"The SOE is Prime Minister Churchill's project. He set it up in 1940 to assist the war effort."

"Am I allowed to ask what it does?"

"Our war defence against the Nazis includes sea blockade and air bombardment. The SOE is our third defence against Hitler's advancement. The SOE subvert and sabotage the enemy in occupied cities. The agents gather information in secret and pass it to our war office in Whitehall. It is extremely valuable work."

I am still unclear about how they operate. "What exactly do the agents do?"

"A number of things, actually. They deliver and transport explosive materials and devices in occupied countries. They provide money to our partners and establish networks. They have brought back details of factories where British agents will find sympathizers and lists of French Resistance supporters. They have secured ration books, permits and details of train services." He pauses to let me absorb his words.

"They do all that without getting caught by the enemy?"

"There are many French people willing to help us sabotage the Germans. They provide safe houses for our agents and letter boxes for couriers. Farmers and villagers agree to have arms dropped in their fields and hide them in their barns until they are collected by agents. Some of our biggest supporters are French railway, postal and factory workers. They take great risks to assist our agents."

Our long-serving postman's face flashes up in my mind. I wonder if he assists the SOE agents. Would he be brave enough to join the French Resistance?

"It seems dangerous," I finally say.

"It is and very few people can do it because it is vital that the SOE agents in France blend in as French citizens. Their French has to be immaculate as well as their knowledge of local customs. Any hint of Britishness would betray them as agents which would mean capture and certain death."

I now realize why I am here. My French language

expertise was noted that day I was interviewed by the woman who worked for the WAAF. I wait for the words I know are coming.

"You could be an SOE agent, if you wish."

Although I expected the offer, it still hits me with a force that sends my mind reeling. This important man believes I could be an SOE agent. I could be one of Churchill's special recruits who are vital to defeating the Nazis. This is the kind of work that Vilayat and I dreamed about doing, but never thought possible.

"Me?" I ask.

"Yes, *if* we give you the job, you could work as a secret radio operator helping the Resistance to sabotage the Germans. You could send secret messages to head office in London."

My mind is made up. "I would like to do it."

I can tell from the expression on his face that I have shocked him with my willingness to accept the job.

"Think about it first," he says hurriedly. "This is not something to be rushed into. Lives depend on SOE agents and the slightest mistake can be fatal." He pauses. "We have a real shortage of radio operators and you would be the first female radio operator in the field. It is dangerous work. You would have to carry a wireless set with you to do your work and the possibility of capture from the Germans is high. The wireless set will betray you if are caught."

I nod but he continues.

"As an SOE agent you will wear no uniform. Without a uniform, you will have no protection under international laws of warfare."

"I would still like to do it, sir."

He closes the file on his desk. "Speak to your family first and then give me your answer."

I think of Amma. Will I be able to persuade her? I thank Mr Jepson, gather my things and leave the room.

*

That night there is a chilly wind howling outside and the old single pane windows of Amma's living room are failing to keep the draught out. I decided to cycle over and stay the night so that I could tell her of my new plans. We are both huddled on the sofa, a warm shawl around each of our shoulders. Amma also has a blanket to cover her legs. She looks tired from her shift at the hospital and I think twice about bringing up the subject. It is Amma who remembered that my interview was today. "How did the meeting go at the War Commission?"

Her question throws me and I make an effort to keep my voice casual.

"They have asked me to join the FANY," I reply. "It's the First Aid Nursing Yeomanry." This is the organization that Selwyn informed me is used by all female agents as a front for their work. No one suspects nurses who have to travel to aid the injured. The lie comes easily but I can't help but feel a little guilty for misleading my amma.

Amma's smile is broad. "That's wonderful, Noor. You're going back to nursing. I knew you would become bored with all that operating work and plotting planes."

I'm not sure how to reply, so I stay silent.

"Where will you be based?" she asks. "I hope not too far from me."

"Well, that's just it," I say slowly. "The FANY require all the nurses to travel around, sometimes even abroad."

"Abroad!?"

Ah, the reaction I've been waiting for.

"Amma," I adopt the patient voice I often used with Khair growing up. "Nurses have to go wherever injured troops are. This is a world war. Our men are fighting in lands near and far."

I feel terrible for not telling her the exact truth, but I know that I cannot in all honesty inform Amma that I am about to be enlisted as a spy for Churchill. The work is far too dangerous for her liking and she would never let me leave.

"It offers more money than I currently get in the WAAF and it will help pay for Khair's medical training fees. You, me and Vilayat promised that we would pay the cost."

Amma nods slowly. "Yes, there is that but, Noor, I'd rather you weren't travelling abroad and—"

"Amma," I interrupt gently. "I have to take this opportunity."

She manages a teary smile and squeezes my hand. "Whatever makes you happy, dear."

The next day I pause in front of the red postbox, a letter clutched in my hand. I'd written it just after Amma had left for her shift at the hospital. In it, I conformed to Selwyn that I would like to accept the invitation to become an SOE agent.

I am in no doubt that if I post this letter my life will change for ever. Taking a deep breath, I push the envelope through the gap.

Chapter 8

Spy School

Before I begin my agent training, I swap my blue Air Force uniform for the khaki dress of the First Aid Nursing Yeomanry (FANY). Though I don't have an official uniform as an agent (that would rather give it away!) the FANY uniform is the perfect disguise for female agents. People don't question why nurses are on their own, far away from home, and let them get on with their business without asking too many questions.

I've signed the Official Secrets Act and I did so with pride and without hesitation. From now on, everything that I hear and see must be kept secret at all times. Failure to do this will mean that I have committed treason against King and Country.

On the morning I travel to Guildford station for my

training, the air is cold and I tuck my hands deep in my pockets. The breeze whips my khaki coat as I look up and down the platform, struggling to get my bearings. Another young woman, dressed identically to me, catches my eye. Something tells me she's not a nurse either.

"Hello."

"You're not by any chance heading towards Wanborough Manor, are you?" she asks.

"Yes I am. Shall we walk together?" I extend my hand. "I'm Nora."

Her grip is firm. "Yolande Beekman."

We fall into step to make our way to the place known as Special Training School Five that has been set up by the SOE.

"How did you get chosen for this role?" I ask.

"My father was Swiss-French and I can speak German and French," she explains.

"Ah, yes," I laugh. "Fluent French seems to be the main qualification for this job. That's why I was selected too."

She takes a quick glance at me. "I hope you don't mind me saying so, but you don't seem very French."

"Yes, I get that a lot." I shrug. "My mother is an American and my father was an Indian. I was born in Russia, brought up in France and now fighting for the British."

"So that explains your accent," she says. "It's a

combination of all those countries."

"What about you?" I want to know more about her. "How did they recruit you?"

"Through the WAAF," she whispers, looking over her shoulder to make sure no one can overhear us. "I joined after my marriage broke down."

"I'm sorry to hear that."

Yolande shrugs. "We married very young and it wasn't meant to be. You know, I can't wait for this war to be over."

"Me too ... ooh look!" I marvel at Wanborough Manor as it comes into view. "A Tudor mansion. I love these old English houses from the time of Queen Elizabeth's reign, especially the black and white walls and steep roofs."

Yolande shares my admiration. "Before the war we'd never have been allowed inside. But now all these castles and palaces of the aristocracy are being used to train agents."

"Well, we're all in it together."

"For King and Country."

*

My bones ache like they have never done before and I find myself longing for a hot soak in the bath. The training here is at a level which makes the WAAF physical exercises I hated feel like a walk in the park. It is so difficult. Every morning we have a ten-minute run and then lessons on handling guns, grenades and explosives. I've handled every type of war weapon, from a small pistol which I can curve into the palm of my hand, to sub-machine guns. I worry about what Abba would say, if he were still alive. I hope he would see that it was necessary, and understand that I would only ever use violence as a last resort.

My colleagues have had training to jump out of planes with parachutes – but not me. I failed my medical on the grounds of poor feet, though I have no idea what that means. How do I have poor feet? I can run really fast, which is a requirement for this job, so my feet can't be that bad! Though I'm disappointed that I can't take part in this area of the training, it gives me more time to practise my map reading, which I'm getting very good at. I suppose that should help too, even if it is not as exciting as jumping out of planes.

*

"Are you ready to train as Special Operator Agents?"

I can't help the small smile at the words of the instructor standing at the front of the class. The tall, lean man with the balding head could be mistaken for a professor at any university. Yet, here he is, probably a veteran in his field, teaching us young recruits how to work in secret.

"Being an agent requires a few basic rules," he begins.

"Observe them and you will survive to return home. Ignore them and you might never make it out of enemy territory."

I glance around at the other trainee agents. Each one has a look of pure concentration on their faces. Yolande's pen is poised to take down notes. I pick up my own, turning my attention back to the instructor.

"Rule number one: your identity must always remain a secret. If it is compromised, then you are compromised. Live, eat and breathe your cover name. Is that clear?"

Some heads nod.

"Understood?" he snaps, unimpressed.

All of us nod.

"Rule number two: you must find secure places to meet. These are known as 'safe houses'. Never get comfortable, because it can be compromised at any time. You must always remain on the move."

I begin to take notes.

*

A few weeks later I am moved on again. This time to Thame Park in Oxfordshire, where I attend an advanced signal course.

I've always had high marks at Morse code, but they want me to increase my speed. By the time I leave a few weeks later my speed is up to eighteen words per minute to send and twenty-two words per minute to receive.

I am the fastest radio operator currently available to Prime Minister Churchill.

Chapter 9

"The End of the Beginning"

I wave one last time at Amma. We have said our goodbyes outside the home she now rents in Gordon Square in Euston. This is the same square where my parents lived when I was a baby. It must have so many memories for Amma, and I wish we had more time to share these stories together. Vilayat is away with the navy and I am disappointed not have been able to say goodbye.

Khair has a break from her medical course in Edinburgh and is accompanying me on the journey from Euston Square to Baker Street. When we board our train, the carriage is empty except for one man sitting at the other end.

"How long will you be gone?" Khair asks.

"I'm not sure," I reply vaguely. "A few months."

"But you haven't said specifically where you are going."

I roll my eyes. "You know that's classified information, Khair."

"What does that even mean?" Her voice is tinged with frustration. It's obvious this has been on her mind for a while now, but she probably didn't want to voice her concerns in front of Amma.

"It means I'm not allowed to tell you," I insist gently.

Khair folds her arms. "Amma thinks you're going to Africa."

"She may be right," I say, hoping it's enough to stop Khair from pursuing answers.

"So you *are* going to Africa to work as a nurse?"

"It's classified," I repeat, my eyes on the only other person in the carriage.

He is standing by the doors, ready to disembark as the train pulls out of the tunnel and into the next station. There are a few passengers scattered along the platform, but none that board our carriage. With no one to overhear us, I turn to Khair and speak seriously.

"Now listen, I've got something to tell you."

Khair looks at me with the trusting eyes of a younger sibling. How can I say this without giving her an idea of what my future holds? I plunge in, hoping she will just trust me.

"If you ever get called up by the War Office or any

83

other government department to do liaison work, you must say no."

She blinks. "What? Why?"

"Please don't ask me to explain more than I'm able to. Just remember that if the War Office say they are impressed with your French-speaking skills and links with France, and they have a special role for you, then you must say that you are not interested."

"But ... if I can be of help—" Khair begins.

I raise my hand to cut her off, as if she's still a child. "Just say no. Our brothers are doing their bit in the French Resistance and the navy. I am also leaving on an assignment. Who knows what danger we will face? You must be the one to remain here to look after Amma. She will not be able to cope on her own."

Though I feel the hypocrisy in my words, they are enough to convince Khair and she nods in agreement. I squeeze her hand as relief floods through me. I will offer my own life willingly to the war, but I do not want my sister in any danger. For the first time, I feel a sense of guilt as I am given a glimpse into how Amma must be feeling about my brothers and me putting ourselves in danger.

The train pulls into Baker Street station and we make our way up to the exit. It is time to say goodbye, for now. I hug my baby sister, not wanting to let her go. A part of me wants to remain with Amma and Khair, and look after them like I have done so since Abba died, but I know the job I am going to do is even more important.

"Be good," I say, clasping my sister's hands one last time, before turning to walk away. To keep the pain of the parting at bay, I think of the speech that Churchill delivered last year after a success against the Nazis. I found his words so inspirational that I memorized them. They give me courage now.

> *"Now this is not the end.*
> *It is not even the beginning of the end.*
> *But it is perhaps the end of the beginning."*

Chapter 10

Field Tests

May 1943

I am in the heart of a picturesque village in Beaulieu, Hampshire, and a man is trailing me. He is dressed in a long overcoat and hat, and has been following me for at least ten minutes. No matter which postbox or car I scoot behind, I am never out of his line of sight. I need to lose him!

I am taking part in one of the last exercises of SOE training before I go abroad, and must lose this stalker in order to pass the test. *What to do? Think, Noor, think!*

I need to blend into a crowd. Glancing around, I spot a greengrocer with some customers inside. I cross the road quickly and enter the shop. The bell at the top of the door announces my entry but nobody pays me any attention. Through the window I can see that the agent has tucked himself behind a delivery van. Perhaps I could trick him by changing my appearance? I slip off my green coat and bundle it under my arms. I know it's not enough to disguise me. I need something else to make me inconspicuous. I glance around and spot a woman's wide-brimmed hat on a coat peg near the counter. It must belong to the owner. Sidling up, I take it down and slip it on to my head. I still don't think it will be enough to lose the man, though.

"Hush, little angel, please don't cry."

I glance over my shoulder at a young woman trying to soothe the child on her hips. Despite her comforting coos, the baby already has tears running down his cheeks. I see my chance and walk over.

"Oh, how old?"

"Eight months," replies the mother distractedly.

"Would you like a hand with your shopping?" I pick up the brown parcels from the counter before she can object. "Here, let me get the door for you."

She looks flustered but walks through. "Oh, thank you."

"I love babies," I gush, keeping my head down as I step out on to the street. "Though I'm sure it's very difficult."

"It is." The mother suddenly looks tearful. "I'm on my own. His father is away fighting. My Freddie hasn't even met his son yet."

"I'm sure he will be back very soon," I say in what I hope is a soothing voice. "You've just got to hang on."

We carry on talking until we reach the end of the street. I glance over my shoulder but the streets are empty.

Yes! I've lost the agent.

"Where do you live?" I ask.

"Not far," she says.

I smile. "I'll walk you to your door."

The baby has quietened down and we walk in silence for a while longer before we arrive at her home.

"Thank you so much," she says.

"You're very welcome." I place her parcels by the door and continue down the street. There is no sign of the man with the overcoat and hat, so I head to the finishing point – the Queen Elizabeth pub.

"Well done, Nora," the training officer says with a smile when I walk in. "You've given your pursuer the slip."

"Thank you, sir."

"You can head back to headquarters with Cecily here." He points to a girl sitting at a side table. "Another one who aced her test."

I smile at Cecily and she gives me a thumbs up sign. We've been training together since we arrived and she's great fun to be around. I walk up to where she sits.

"I need to make a quick stop first," I say. "Do you want to come with me?"

She gets to her feet. "Sure," she says. "Where to?"

"I just need to return the hat on my head to its rightful owner."

Chapter 11

Poison and a Pistol

"Do you know who I am?"

I nod. The man sitting opposite me is Maurice Buckmaster, the leader of the French section of the SOE. He shuffles some papers on the desk. I hold my breath.

"These are your progress reports," he says. "You must know that the final decision to send an agent into the field is mine."

I exhale. "Yes, sir."

His gaze is steady. "I have been watching you for some time, Nora. You are a little unusual in our ranks. Born in Moscow, raised in France and of American and Indian descent. Quite the internationalist, aren't you?"

"I suppose so, sir."

"You are the daughter of a Muslim Sufi preacher – Mr Inayat Khan who believed in non-violence."

"Yes, sir, my abba was a peaceful man."

"What would you say was the most important lesson that he taught you?"

"Truth," I reply simply. "He believed in always telling the truth."

The silence that follows stretches into a few seconds. I return his gaze, wondering what is going through this powerful man's mind.

"Nazis," he finally says extremely slowly, "are the worst type of enemy to encounter in the battlefield. Be in no doubt that you will be entering into a psychological struggle with them. They will be ruthless in their pursuit of you. It will be a cat-and-mouse game – they will hunt and you will be hunted."

I nod. "I have prepared myself to face them, sir."

My hands are shaking in my lap.

"Nora, I am going to send you to France."

Oh!

"You are the fastest and best transmitter we have. I do not share my colleagues' reservations about you. My instincts tell me that you will cope when you find yourself in the middle of the battle. Selwyn Jepson, you remember him? He was the first to interview you."

"Yes, sir."

"He agrees with me," he says. "I have complete confidence in your strength of character and positive attitude. I believe you will do us proud."

I cannot believe the praise. "I will not let you down, sir."

"Very good." He shuffles some pages on his desk. "Your codename to members of the French section of the SOE will be Madeleine, your cover name will be Jeanne-Marie Renier. You will use Madeleine to identify yourself to other SOE agents, and Jeanne-Marie will be your new civilian identity. You must not get the two confused. Understood?"

"Yes, sir."

"Good. I see in your form that you wish to be situated in Paris?"

I want to go back to the city I grew up in, even if it has been transformed by the war.

"You still insist on it, Nora?"

"Yes, sir. I know the city very well and will be most effective there."

"You do realize it will be full of the Gestapo?" He is referring to Hitler's secret police who have the power to send anyone they arrest to the prison camps. "They will be on every corner."

"I do and I believe I will manage."

"Very well."

"Thank you, sir."

He pulls open a drawer, lifts something out and slides it across the desk. I stare at it. It is a small pistol. "You will carry the pistol on your journey to France. If your arrival goes according to plan, then you must bury the pistol in the ground. Get rid of it as soon as you can because possession of it will get you into trouble."

I nod, a little unsure why I need to carry it if I need to get rid of it so quickly.

"If, however," he says slowly, "your landing is ambushed by the enemy then you must use it to save yourself."

A shiver runs down my spine. I am the daughter of a pacifist – how can I take a life with my own hands? Maurice seems to read my mind.

"You will have to use the pistol to protect yourself; otherwise the Nazis will capture, torture and kill you. It is you or them. Survival is key for all SOE agents. Churchill is banking on you to help save us all. Without your work, and that of other SOE agents, we will not be able to defend this land. You must subvert and sabotage the Nazis on the continent in preparation for our own attack."

I nod quickly. "Of course."

He is quiet, assessing me with his blue eyes.

"I am committed to the mission, sir."

He seems reassured and moves on to the next part of his talk. "You will be given four pills before you depart. The first one will induce sleep and it is to be used in an enemy's tea or coffee."

That doesn't seem as difficult as using a pistol. I nod.

"The second pill is a stimulant. It is called Benzedrine. Only take it if you find yourself falling asleep when you need to remain awake."

I nod.

"The third pill is to be taken by you if you need to appear ill to get yourself out of a hostile situation. It will mimic a stomach bug and leave you with vomiting and diarrhoea. It might work to divert attention away from you as nobody wants to be around a sick person. Remember, it will make you physically ill, so only take it if you really need to."

"Yes, sir."

"The fourth pill…" He trails off in hesitation.

I raise my brows. "Sir?"

"The fourth and final pill contains cyanide. It will be your final option if you are captured and do not wish to be interrogated by the enemy." He pauses to give me a moment for his words to settle in. "One bite and you will be dead within minutes. But do not forget, the pill has to be *bitten*. It will be completely ineffective if you swallow it."

I hide my shock. "Understood."

"Nora, I want you to remember this. Capture does not always mean the end. If you think you can survive the imprisonment and possible torture, then live through it."

All I can do is nod.

"I have one more thing for you. It is a gift given to all SOE agents. In your darkest moments and in your times of fear, it is to remind you that we at home are thinking of you." His hand reaches back into the drawer to pull out a round shiny object. "We are praying for you. We are relying on you. We are with you in spirit."

I only realize what it is when he slides it across the desk.

A gold compact mirror.

"The men get lighters," he says with a small smile.

I pick it up gently. "Thank you, sir. I appreciate it."

"Not as much as we appreciate what you are doing for our country. God be with you, Agent Khan."

*

The room is lit by a single lamp on the bedside table. I fasten the button of my green coat ready for inspection. It is nearly time for me to leave England for France on my mission as an SOE agent. I smile at Vera Watkins. She works for Maurice

Buckmaster and it is her job to deliver me to the airfield for my departure.

"I need to check your pockets one last time," she says.

I stand completely still with my arms held out. Her hands search for English cigarettes, bus tickets and English money in my coat. When nothing is found she looks up at me and smiles. "Very good. Nothing to betray you to the enemy."

Vera then digs into her own pocket to hand me a package. It is small enough to fit into the palm of my hand. I guess the contents; the pills for the four possible situations.

"You know which pill does what?"

I nod, slipping the package into my handbag.

"You have your pistol?"

I pat the handbag. "Already packed."

"And your French ID and ration card?"

I nod.

"Shall we go over your cover story one last time?"

I nod again.

"What is your cover name?"

"Jeanne-Marie Renier."

"What do you do?"

"I am a children's nurse."

"When is your birthday?"

"25th April."

"What is your father's name and what did he do?"

"Auguste Renier. He was a professor of Philosophy at Princeton University in America."

"When did he die?"

"He was killed in the Great War."

"And your mother?"

"Ray Baker, an American woman. She returned to America just before 1940 when France fell to the Germans." We have decided to use a cover story that has elements of truth, so that it'll be easier to remember.

Vera smiles. "Good. Now codename?"

"Madeleine."

"Madeleine is only to be used with other SOE agents, don't forget."

There's a knock on the door and I take a deep breath. So does Vera. She looks just as nervous as I feel. How many agents has she sent into enemy territory? How many have ever returned?

Chapter 12

Long Live Paris

June 1943

The full moon is a beautiful sight. It shines brightly overhead as the car pulls up on the tarmac. I am to fly with three other agents who are already waiting. I smile as I recognize one of them. It's Cecily from my training in Beaulieu. She came with me to return the hat I borrowed when I needed to disguise myself in a field test. I'm so glad there is someone I already know on this flight. We exchange a quick hug and then I step forward to shake hands with the two strangers. "Nora Baker."

"I'm Charles Skepper," says the man.

The third agent smiles. "Diana Rowden. Can you believe the size of this thing?"

I turn my gaze to the plane. How is this little toy-like structure going to get across the Channel? It's just as well that our luggage, including my radio set, is going to be parachuted into France at a later date.

"It's called a Lysander," Charles says. "It seats a maximum of four people and can only travel up to two hundred miles an hour. That's its main advantage."

Really? Lack of speed is an advantage?

"Yes, it is," he laughs at my expression. "It's so slow that the German fighter planes fail to notice it when they whizz past."

"How marvellous," Diana says. "They really can't see it?"

"Only in daylight which is why we're flying at night."

Vera taps my shoulder. "It's time to say goodbye."

I hug her tightly. "Thank you for all your help."

"God be with you, Nora."

Legs trembling, I climb the ladder to board the plane. We settle into our seats and strap in. A few more minutes and we're taxiing down the runway, before soaring into the sky. We talk and joke once we're in the air, exhilarated by the thought of the adventure. Unsurprisingly, we are nervous too. We are flying into great danger, but what choice do we really have?

The world cannot be left to Hitler. He will strip it of colour and leave it in darkness. Instead, we fight for *liberté* – for freedom.

Five hours pass and the plane finally comes to a

skidding halt. We have landed in a country occupied by the enemy, we must hurry. Once the ladder is thrown over the side, we descend as quickly as we can before coming face-to-face with five passengers down on the landing field.

We move quickly aside to allow them to board the Lysander, where they will begin their journey back to Britain. They look like they are desperate to flee. Perhaps they have seen horrible things and only just escaped by the skin of their teeth. Within ten minutes the tiny plane has turned around and is taxiing off. I breathe deeply, trying to calm my nerves.

The four of us cross quickly to the side of the runway. My eyes scan the surrounding area. There is nothing out there but trees in the distance. This is a completely isolated spot with no houses, no barns – nothing.

Suddenly, two men step forward causing me to jump slightly.

They must be the agents assigned by London to meet us. "I am Henri Déricourt," says the taller one in French. "This is my assistant Rémy Clément. This way, please. We have bikes for you."

I remind myself that from this moment onwards, we must only speak in French in case we are overheard.

Once they have led us to the bikes, I exchange quick hugs with Cecily and Diana.

"Take care of yourself, Nora," Cecily says. She and Charles are heading to the south of France together.

"And you, too." I turn to Diana. "Where are you going?"

"I'm heading to south-east of Dijon, near the Jura mountains," Diana replies. "Take care, Noor. You are going to the most dangerous place."

Though I know it will be dangerous, the thought of going to Paris gives me a little buzz. I'm looking forward to returning to the city where I was raised. Soon, they are all gone, except Rémy.

"Madeleine," he says. "I'll be travelling to Paris on the same train as you, but it's not safe for us to ride together so I'll head off first and see you on the platform."

I watch him cycle into the night and then turn to complete my most immediate task. Walking over to the grass, I pull the pistol out of my handbag, ready to bury it. Vera's advice had been to get rid of it as soon as possible.

"Being found in possession of it in a Nazi stop and search will put you in real danger," she'd said.

I dig the earth with my bare hands. As it is summer, the ground is not as hard as it would be in winter, but it is still a difficult task. What I wouldn't do for my trusted ice-clearing shovel back at Fazal Manzil. The hole dug, I place the pistol inside and quickly sweep the earth over it, trying to memorize the exact spot so I can dig up the pistol for when I return to England. Perhaps I will be picked up from the same place by another Lysander plane.

Climbing on to the bike, I pedal as fast as I can, following the path that Rémy took moments before. Despite the full moon, the night is eerily still and silent and relief floods through me as a church spire appears, quickly followed by rows of roofs as the rest of the village comes into view. The railway station must be close.

I notice Rémy on the platform but do not acknowledge him. The nerves are back and I want to make sure I am heading in the right direction. I pull the train map out of my bag to study it. When I look up I see Rémy frowning at me. My heart skips a beat. Why is he doing that? Then I realize that I may well be giving the impression of a stranger who is lost. Not appearing confident would arouse suspicion in any nearby Nazi soldier, or even a French citizen sympathetic to their side. I hurriedly stuff the map back into my bag as the train pulls into the station.

I notice that Rémy boards a separate carriage to me. That's just as well as I found his earlier scowling a little intimidating. Taking a seat by the window, I decide to do nothing but stare at the passing countryside in all its shadowy glory. At least this way I can't be accused of looking out of the ordinary.

Hours later, I am blessed to witness the most beautiful sunrise overlooking the French countryside. How I've missed France!

The serenity I feel soon evaporates when the train chugs into Paris in the late afternoon. I glance around the platform as I step down to see if I can spot Rémy. He is nowhere to be seen. Well, I suppose I'm finally on my own. I walk quickly out of the station on to the street and it hits me that this is not the same Paris I grew up in. There is an odd atmosphere in the air. I walk past people who refuse to make eye contact with me. There is no hello, no smile. It's as if there's a cloud of fear. Like an invisible chemical that can't be seen but can be felt.

I turn a corner and almost gasp out loud. Four Nazi soldiers are walking straight towards me. I lower my head so I don't have to meet their eyes, and they pass me seconds later with zero interest in me.

This first glimpse of the enemy has unnerved me and I take a deep breath to compose myself. I hadn't expected to react like that. Of course I knew I would see Nazi soldiers on the streets, but expecting it and actually seeing them in the flesh are two different things.

I bury the gloomy feeling and focus on finding the safe house. I have memorized the instructions. I need to get to apartment 16E, in building number 40 on a street called *Rue Erlanger*. It is the house of Emile Henri Garry.

Perhaps I should buy some flowers for Emile.

Soon after, I knock on 16E ready with my password.

The door is swung open by a young man. He stares at me and I glance over his shoulder. Where's my contact? "Mademoiselle, won't you come in," he says.

I step over the threshold, flowers in my hand.

He introduces me to a pretty girl in his living room. "This is my fiancée, Marguerite."

"Hello," I greet, wondering why she is looking at me and then back at the man. Does she expect me to give her the flowers? I would, but they are for my contact.

"Please sit," the man invites.

I perch down on the chair, glancing around for the old lady. Where is she? Have I come to the wrong place?

"Cigarette?" Marguerite offers.

I take it and the man leans forward to light it. We smoke in silence and I notice the couple exchange another odd look. Something is wrong.

Marguerite suddenly jumps to her feet. "I will make some coffee."

The man and I sit in silence until I can bear it no longer. "No old lady here?"

He shakes his head, looking a little puzzled.

I memorized the address so there's no way to check this place against a piece of paper. What if I remembered it wrong? There is only one thing left to do. I take a deep breath and deliver the password. "I have come on behalf of your friend Antoine for news on the building society."

He looks positively delighted at my words. Leaning forward he says, "The business is in hand."

Yes!

He has delivered his own password. This man is my contact. Now why ever did I think my contact was an old lady?

"I thought you would never speak the password," he says, a smile crinkling his eyes.

"I was expecting an old lady. I even bought the flowers for her."

"I think you were confused by my first name Emile. Everybody knows me as Henri Garry."

We are both laughing when Marguerite walks back into the room with a tray.

"Our agent is here!" Henri Garry jumps to his feet to make space on the small coffee table. He then turns and half bows in my direction. "Madeleine."

Marguerite joins in with the laughter. "Well, that is good news. Here," she hands me a cup. "Try this, although I will tell you in advance that you will have tasted much, much better."

I take a sip. She is right – it tastes awful but I don't want to be rude so I gulp it down.

"Will you stay for dinner?"

The thought of food makes my tummy rumble. "Thank you. I haven't really eaten."

I explain that I was unsure how to use the French ration card and didn't want to bring undue attention to myself if I got it wrong. Marguerite cooks a simple meal and we settle down at the table, talking of the changes that have come over the city since the Nazis arrived.

"Is it true that Jewish people are being forced to wear yellow stars?" I ask. I had heard a rumour about this back in London.

"Yes, it's true," Henri Garry confirms. "Many of them have been rounded up and sent to concentration camps in Poland and Germany."

"Concentration camps?" I ask.

"That's what they call the prison camps now. So many people crammed into prisons because they belong to the Jewish race or because they are political prisoners who disagree with the ideas of German superiority. It is said that once a person is sent to a concentration camp, he or she will never be seen again."

I shudder at the image Henri Garry is painting. All those poor people locked away through no fault of their own.

"What about their businesses and homes?"

"All grabbed by Germans and the French collaborators. It pains me when I think of how people betrayed their Jewish neighbours to the Nazis."

"Oh, that's terrible," I say. I cannot imagine any of our neighbours in Suresnes doing the same thing.

"Some French people are eager to please the occupiers," Marguerite says, shaking her head sadly. "And the Jews are not the only ones being targeted by the Nazis. The Roma, the disabled and the homosexuals too. Being in the Resistance means we hear leaked news. The world doesn't know the full horrors of what the Nazis are inflicting in the concentration camps but we know. It is why we are so determined to end the darkness. Why we see it as our duty in the name of humanity to help bring an end to Hitler's rampage."

I am silent as I absorb Marguerite's words. It is even worse than I imagined it would be.

"You will find Paris very different to how you left it," Henri Garry says. "Before the occupation the words on everyone's lips were '*sales Boches*' – dirty Germans. Now they say '*sales Anglais*' – dirty English. We do not know who to trust any more."

We finish our meal in gloomy silence and then move over to the sofa.

"Let me tell you about our work," Henri Garry says. "The agents are all divided up into groups called circuits. I am the head of our circuit – it's called Cinema. Our circuit is part of a bigger circuit called Prosper, which is very successful. As a radio operator your job will be to send messages to London and receive them. We sabotage power stations and attack Nazi trains carrying equipment and arms in an attempt to weaken them. We are succeeding in accomplishing what Churchill ordered. We are sabotaging and subverting."

I nod slowly. "So it's working."

"It's not easy," Henri Garry warns. "It's very dangerous. A betrayal or mistake of any kind immediately leads to capture. And capture means death."

The smile is wiped off my face and the words send a shiver down my spine.

"Madeleine," Henri Garry says gently. I think he has sensed my fear. "As long as we are all vigilant, we will be fine. Vigilance is key."

"Yes," I say with a brightness I do not feel.

Henri Garry is about to add something else when a yawn escapes me. Suddenly, it is hard to keep my eyes open. The food in my belly and the comfort of the sofa is making me drowsy.

"You are tired, Madeleine," Henri Garry states the obvious.

Another yawn. "I'm sorry! You must think I'm being so rude."

"Nonsense," Henri Garry smiles. "You've had quite a journey. You will sleep here tonight."

Chapter 13

Codename Madeleine

The sun's rays feel glorious on my skin as I sit outside a café, sipping a cold drink in the summer heat. A meeting has been set up by Henri Garry for me with a radio operator who goes by the codename Archambaud, so that I can transmit my first message at the allotted time. I glance around. It has taken a few days but I've managed to take this new Paris in my stride. Well, all except the Nazi soldiers whose steel-capped boots clink-clank along the cobbled streets as a reminder that they are never far away.

Suddenly, a shadow looms over me, blocking out the warm sunlight. I didn't even notice him approach. I look up and gasp with surprise. It's my childhood friend Gilbert. What's he doing here? The last time I saw him was outside Fazal Manzil when my family and I were fleeing Paris.

"Gilbert," I say. "I didn't expect to see you here."

"Archambaud, actually." He steps to the side, exposing the sun again.

I shield my eyes with my hand as I gaze up at him, absorbing his words. Finally, it dawns on me.

"You are the radio operator I'm supposed to meet?"

"The very one," Gilbert smiles and takes a seat. "How are you, Noor? Or should I call you Madeleine?"

"Actually, I'm Jeanne-Marie, the nurse," I retort playfully, my voice barely above a whisper.

He grins. "It must be confusing to have so many names."

We chat about our families and old school friends before he turns to work.

"So, your radio set hasn't arrived yet, has it?"

I smooth the flowery dress that I've borrowed from Marguerite. "Neither have my clothes."

"Don't worry; you can use my set to transmit your arrival message to London. We should get going soon." He points at my lemonade. "Finish it."

I dutifully raise the glass to my lips and listen as he talks.

"I transmit from the grounds of the Natural College of Agriculture. I am the radio operator for the head of the Bricklayer circuit, France Antelme. You won't be able to miss him. He's a tall Mauritian man who is never seen

111

without a purple beret on his head. You can meet him and other circuit members when they get together later today at the college."

"Sounds good." I say, lowering my empty glass on the table.

"We should leave now." He scrapes his chair back and stands up.

I nod, feeling a little thrill.

An hour later I find myself surrounded by green plants, small and big, and sweating from the humid atmosphere of the greenhouse at the Natural College of Agriculture. Gilbert climbs up on to some boxes and then disappears behind. I wipe the sweat off my brow.

"Here we go." Gilbert emerges from behind the boxes with a suitcase. "The set is inside. It's a bit heavy. Will you be able to manage?"

I flex my arm muscles which are really non-existent and laugh. "I think so."

Gilbert grins and pulls out the twenty-metre aerial. "You have to hang this as high as possible so you can get a signal."

I don't bother to inform him that I received the training back in England and instead watch silently as he climbs on to a stool to dangle the aerial between two branches of a small tree.

"This," he says from high up, "is the most dangerous part.

You need to make sure the aerial is not spotted by the Nazis."

"Noted," I call out.

"But," Gilbert jumps off the stool, "it's not just the Nazis you have to be careful of. Remember, that there are some French people that support them. They can report you at any time. Be wary of everyone. Trust no one."

I nod solemnly and approach the set. I tune to the right frequency and, as I begin to type, I remember the girls' nickname for me back at WAAF training – "Bang Away Lulu". I was suffering from chilblains and had sore fingers then, but now my heavy-handedness comes from nerves.

MADELEINE HAS ARRIVED

My first message to London as an SOE agent is delivered.

"All done!" Gilbert yanks down the aerial.

With the set safely hidden away, Gilbert and I make our way to the main building of the college. Some of the other agents from our circuits are already inside this rather grand structure which looks like a palace from the outside, and I am nervous about being introduced to them.

"Welcome, Madeleine," a middle-aged man says, smiling at me. "I'm Professor Balachowsky, a member of Prosper and a biologist at this college."

I am whisked around the room to meet a number of agents and Resistance fighters, all working against the Nazi occupation of France. I smile at them all, aware that it will take me a while to remember their names.

"Hello, you must be our new addition."

I gaze up at the tall man who has spoken. From his height, and the purple beret perched atop his head, I gather this must be France Antelme.

"Pleased to meet you," I reply. "I'm Madeleine."

He moves on to greet the next person and I look around, feeling a little out of place. It's hard being the new person in the room.

"Time for tea," someone calls out.

Happy to have something to keep my hands busy, I offer to help. The tea tray is passed to me and I pour the milk into the first cup. By the time I'm on my third one, there is silence all around. I look up to see everyone's eyes fixed on me and some faces are even frowning. With a trembling hand, I place the teapot down and look to Gilbert for explanation. He gives me a sympathetic smile.

Madame Balachowsky approaches me. "In France," she says, taking over the tea tray, "the milk is poured last. How did you forget? Only the British pour the milk first."

"I'm so sorry," I whisper, wishing the earth would open

up to swallow me whole. These agents must think I am naive and untrained.

"Easy mistake," Madame Balachowsky says, handing me a cup. "But don't do it again. It could betray you and the rest of us to the Nazis. It's the little habits that can give us away. Remember, you must be Madeleine. Forget Nora Baker and her habits."

I gulp down my tea. It is scorching hot, but nothing compared to the heat I feel from the embarrassment. Just at that moment, Professor Balachowsky calls me over and I follow him into the hallway, the teacup and saucer clattering in my trembling hand. I steal a glance at the professor, noting that the lines on his forehead are deeply furrowed.

"I believe this is yours, Madeleine."

A gasp escapes me. It is my folder with all my code words. For a moment, I can't imagine how he got hold of it, and then I remember: I left the folder in the hallway when we came in. I only meant to put it down for a few minutes while I darted to use the toilet. I must have forgotten to pick it up.

"This is a very dangerous thing to do," he admonishes. "If the other side were to have come across this information, you would soon be captured or dead – as would the rest of us."

For the second time in the same hour, I wish for the ground to open up and swallow me.

"I ... I'm sorry," I manage. "I didn't mean to ..."

The professor raises a hand to halt my apology. He must see that I am on the verge of tears because his expression changes to look sympathetic rather than stern.

"I urge you to be careful, Madeleine. That is all."

He hands me my folder and disappears into the crowd. At least he didn't shame me in front of everyone.

Come on, Noor, I tell myself. *You need to step up. This will not do.*

I return to the gathering, my folder tucked under my arm. My ears still feel hot from the embarrassment of my mistake. I find a chair in the corner and sit down. No longer in the mood to socialize, I want this evening to end.

Hopefully, the professor hasn't felt the need to inform everybody about my silly mistake. The mistake with the milk and tea was bad enough.

Gilbert pulls up a chair. "I've just received news that your luggage has arrived," he tells me. "But I should warn you that you may not find your belongings to be in the pristine condition that you packed them in. The parachute that was attached to your suitcase collided with a tree – the suitcase flew open and your things were strewn across the French countryside."

My mouth falls open and I can feel the red creep up my

neck to invade my face. Gosh, what else can go wrong today?

"Our agents could leave no evidence of tights and underwear scattered in the fields, so the good news is that they retrieved everything and repacked your suitcase."

My face is now burning hot at the thought of my personal items being pulled out of ditches and tugged down from tree branches. I realize Norman has been holding back laughter and despite my embarrassment, I laugh with him.

Then something more important occurs to me. "And my radio set?"

"They've found it. It's intact. It wasn't safe to bring it over to you now, so it's with some other agents. We'll go get it when the coast is clear."

Chapter 14

The Nazi Swoop

June 1943

The afternoon sun shines down on the park bench. Eyes closed, I tip my head back and allow the warmth to envelope me. For a few minutes I feel free and it is as if this was the old Paris again without the marching soldiers.

I am waiting for Gilbert outside the greenhouse. I sit up at the sound of footsteps, and am surprised to see not Gilbert, but Professor Balachowsky coming towards me, looking upset.

The butterflies in my stomach begin to dance. "What's wrong?"

"We've had some terrible news, Madeleine." He slumps down on to the bench and buries his face in his hands. "They were caught two nights ago."

"Who were?"

"The leader of Prosper and seventeen other agents."

The butterflies collide and crash to the bottom of my tummy.

"They were betrayed." He shakes his head sadly. "How else would the Nazis launch a raid on eighteen agents?"

I suddenly look around in a panicked state. "Was Gilbert captured?"

"Possibly."

My heart bangs in my chest. Gilbert captured? I can't believe that my childhood friend is now a prisoner of the Nazis. What will they do to him?

"Now, Madeleine, you must leave." The professor removes his hands from his face to stare at me intently. "I will bury Gilbert's radio set. You must warn the others and remember to always be alert. There is a traitor amongst us. Someone is betraying us to the Nazis."

I say a hurried goodbye and head off as quickly as I can, though I can't run as fast as I want to for fear of bringing attention to myself. Soon, I am banging on Henri Garry's door and relaying the shocking details to my friends.

Marguerite hands me a glass of water. "Drink."

I gulp it down and collapse on the sofa. This is awful. I've just got here and everyone's being arrested.

"We need to speak with Antelme," Henri Garry says.

Later that evening, Antelme decides that he and I should relocate. "There is a vacant flat in my friend's building. I will move in with her and you can take the empty one. Let's go."

I grab the suitcase that I haven't even unpacked yet to follow Antelme through the dark streets of Paris.

"We need to get your radio set soon, but for now you have to keep your head down. Too many agents have been captured and they are probably being tortured for information as we speak."

Cold ice trickles down my spine. What pain must they be going through right now? What if they reveal Antelme's name? Or my name?

"Here we go." We are outside the new flat. Antelme opens the door with a key and lets me in. "I'm not far – just down the stairs. Will you be OK?"

"Yes," I squeak before locking the door.

As the sun shines through the window the following morning after a disturbed night's sleep, I look around my new studio apartment. It consists of a bed, a table, a couple of chairs, a sink and a stove. Only thin plasterboard provides privacy for the bathroom. This brand-new address should not be on any Nazi watch-list.

Antelme orders me to remain inside for days. It's difficult

to stay holed up in this hot weather, and I fret over what is happening to the other agents. Who has been captured and who is still free?

The loneliness causes me to miss Amma terribly. I write letters to her which will transported by the Lysander plane when I'm finally free to leave the flat. Being back in Paris evokes memories of my childhood in Fazal Manzil. I loved to write poems and stories to cheer everyone up, especially Amma. I remember one poem I wrote for her birthday which made her laugh. It was called *The Birthday Man*.

It began:

I saw the little birthday man,
Skipping 'long the way,
I stopped awhile and listened,
To hear what he would say.
He put his little finger
Upon his little head.
He blew the dandelions, and
Danced around and said,
Why, this is my best birthday,
For on this very day,
The storks brought down a girly,
Whose name is Ora Ray...

On the fifth morning, still holed up in my flat, I pick up pen and paper before clambering back into bed. Perhaps I'll compose a poem about the loneliness that can be felt in your own city when it no longer belongs to you.

Barely a line is written when there is an urgent knock on the door.

I jump up from the bed. Who is that?

"Madeleine, it's me."

I recognize the voice. It's Antelme. I yank open the door to stare up at his shattered face. "What's wrong?"

"I've just got word that more agents have been arrested and a number have been killed," he says. "I also have it on good authority that the Gestapo are looking for me specifically. We must leave Paris. No one is safe." The words pour out of him at an incredible speed in his panic. "I have a friend in another circuit who has a place in Auffargis, about twenty-five miles from here. We can lay low for a while.'"

"Down in the country?"

"Yes, it's also an ideal place for weapons to be parachuted in. Are you coming?"

I grab a few clothes and stuff them in a bag. "I'm ready."

July 1943

Auffargis is a peaceful place in the middle of nowhere, yet there is no sense of calm amongst the agents holed up here. Not long after we arrive, I place a call to Professor Balachowsky for an update on the situation in Paris. His poor wife breaks the dreadful news to me – the professor has been arrested.

Oh no!

I try to keep my voice steady as I ask, "Anyone else?"

"The director of the college and six students. Do not call here again."

The line goes dead.

It's not even lunchtime when Antelme announces that he is returning to London. He thinks the situation is just too dangerous here in Paris. He asks if I will go with him and I'm not sure how to respond. Should I return already? What about Gilbert and the others who have been captured? What about my duty?

"Can I think about it?" I ask.

He tells me I have until the morning to decide.

I go for a walk in the countryside. The fresh air feels good after the high pressure atmosphere of Paris.

Looking up at the night sky, I think of Abba and what he

would want me to do. He was a big believer in doing the right thing. The stories he encouraged me to read as a little girl were all about the greater good and self-sacrifice.

I am reminded of the story of sacrifice from my own family history. The story of my great-great-great-grandfather Tipu Sultan who gave his life for his people. I am his descendant. I have the blood of the tiger.

I make my way back to the house and find Antelme.

"I've made up my mind," I say. "I'm staying."

Antelme nods, not at all surprised by my decision. "In that case let me give you the names of a few people that I trust in Paris. One of them is a Frenchman called Viennot. Look him up, you will always be able to trust him. Other names of agents who have not been compromised are Gieules, and then there is . . ."

I dig out my notebook and write down the names of the people who are carrying on the fight.

Chapter 15

Last Operator Standing

I have returned to Paris. With the help of some other agents, I managed to retrieve my radio set from *Le Mans* where it was hidden. Apparently, it is the last remaining set in Paris. All other sets were confiscated by the Nazis when the radio operators were captured.

I've been advised to keep my head down but I know my duty. I must inform London about the fall of the Prosper circuit.

On a quiet Sunday, just before noon, I find a deserted building and climb up five flights of stairs. Reaching the top, I open the hallway window and poke my head out. The street below is empty. Before the war, that would have been impossible to imagine. The street would be brimming with small children and women going about their business, but not any more.

I wait for a few seconds in case a baker's van comes into view. Gilbert warned me that these innocent-looking vehicles are being used as Nazi spy vans. The equipment inside can capture radio signals, exposing SOE agents to capture and arrest. I strain my ears for the click-clack of approaching Nazi boots on cobbled stones, but hear nothing. Good – the coast seems to be clear.

Clicking the radio set open, I grab the aerial and lean out of the window to hang it on a tree branch. I need to be careful to balance it just right, otherwise it might crash to the ground. The last thing I want to do is damage the set, or worse, draw unwanted attention in my direction. Once everything is set up, I take a deep breath and begin to code:

PROSPER HAS FALLEN.

It only takes a few minutes before a message from London arrives.

THIS IS BUCKMASTER.

I reply:

EVERYONE IS CAPTURED.

I AM LAST RADIO OPERATOR STANDING.

I tap my fingers as I wait.

AGENT YOU ARE IN DANGER.
RETURN TO ENGLAND AT ONCE.
ARRANGE TRANSPORT.

No! He can't be pulling me out now.

SIR, I AM THE LAST OPERATOR LEFT.
I CANNOT LEAVE.
THERE WILL BE NO COMMUNICATION BETWEEN
THE REMAINING AGENTS AND LONDON.

The incoming message says:

MADELEINE, YOU ARE IN CLEAR AND
PRESENT DANGER.

I try again to convince him.

I UNDERSTAND, SIR. BUT I MUST REMAIN.
LET ME DO THIS FOR THE CAUSE.

FOR LIBERTE.

There is a long pause and I fear that I have angered Buckmaster. Perhaps he has stormed off. I glance out of the window to check for a Nazi soldier or van.

It is dangerous for me to spend too long here – I should pack up. I'm just about to swing the aerial off the branch when the radio set beeps with an incoming message.

YOU ARE A SOLDIER, MADELEINE.
I, KING AND COUNTRY THANK YOU FOR
YOUR SERVICE.
CARRY ON.
YOUR SACRIFICE FOR THE COUNTRY WILL BE
REMEMBERED.
MAY GOD BE WITH YOU.

I swing the aerial off the branch just as I hear the growl of a van's engine. I pack my set as fast as I can and bolt down the stairs to the ground floor. There is a crack in the wooden front door and I peep through it. My stomach sinks. I see a bakery van parked right outside. Oh no, that must be the Nazis – they must have captured the signal. But where is the click-clack of their boots? There is neither sight nor sound of the soldiers on the road. Are they still in the van, waiting for me to step outside so they can jump out and grab me? Yes, that's probably the case. What am I to do? I can feel the sweat trickling down my back, making my cotton dress damp. I've just told my commander that I'm the last operator standing. I can't fall within minutes of gaining his permission to continue. I need to find an escape.

I rack my brains and suddenly remember that there is a back door to this building. I noticed it when I was scouting for transmission locations. I've never used it before and there is no better time than now. On tiptoe, I slowly move backwards away from the door. A few more seconds and then I'm out of the back door and into an alley. I look around frantically. Yes, the coast is clear. I walk quickly to my left, take a right turning and then another until I am as far away as I can be from that bakery van.

*

A few weeks later, the SOE agents advise me to move again from my flat. I pack my belongings and make my way to Bois de Boulogne in west Paris. I am grateful for an apartment in such a nice part of the city.

It's after dark when I reach my new place and I pay no

attention to my surroundings. It's only in the morning when I leave the flat to find a local bakery that I realize who my neighbours are.

I'm living in a building full of Nazi officers.

Chapter 16

The Monkey Chief

I glance over my shoulder to check I'm not being followed. I'm so used to doing it now that it's as common as looking left and right when I cross a busy road. I wipe a trickle of sweat off my forehead. It's not just the summer heat which is making me hot and bothered. It's the nerves which come with returning to my childhood home, Suresnes.

Despite the strict instructions in my training that I must never revisit places from my past, I am desperate. I am running out of safe places to transmit my messages from. The Nazi spy vans are everywhere in central Paris, hunting for SOE agents.

I visited our family doctor and his wife at their Paris flat and told them that I needed help to transmit. They gave me permission to use their country house in Marly-le-Roi.

There is a scheduled SOE plan to attack a Nazi goods train of guns that are being transported into Paris. The agents will need weapons and London are ready to parachute these weapons into the French countryside. They had been standing by for coordinates for the drop, and it was my job to transmit the details. I managed to do so from Dr Jourdan's garden two days ago.

I'm aware though that I have to be careful about keeping my movements varied, which is why I've come to Suresnes as a last resort.

My legs feel a bit like jelly when I walk up the hill of my old neighbourhood. The radio set feels heavier with each step I take and I can feel myself getting out of breath. I've been crisscrossing all over Paris to transmit messages to London, carrying my set and outwitting Nazi soldiers, but today feels different.

I know it's because I'm so close to my old home, Fazal Manzil. A few more steps and I'll be able to see it. I catch my breath when its beautiful white walls come into view and ... wait. I spot silhouettes in the top window. There is someone inside Amma's room! I had expected the house to be empty like many that had been abandoned by Parisians when they fled in 1940. Had someone taken over our house? I decide the best thing to do is speak to

132

a neighbour first. The closest house belongs to Amma's friend, Madame Pinchon.

*

"Noor!" Madame Pinchon looks like she has seen a ghost when she opens her front door.

"Hello, Madame Pinchon."

She lets me in and I quickly explain my predicament but Madame is reluctant to help.

"I'm sorry, but it's far too dangerous. The Nazis are everywhere. They've even taken possession of Fazal Manzil."

"What?" I can't believe it! Our beautiful House of Blessing is now occupied by Nazis!?

"I'm afraid so," Madame says. "I'm sorry, Noor. I just can't risk you being here. It would endanger my entire family. You should find another place to do your work."

I walk away, careful not to show any disappointment to Madame Pinchon. Of course, I understand her reluctance to help me. The threat of the Nazis is still very real. I do, however, feel fury at the Nazi invasion of my home, but there is nothing I can do about that.

And yet, I can't give up now I'm here. I need to urgently send my messages to London. They need those coordinates as soon as possible. And then it hits me. *Of course!* I should go and visit my childhood friend, Raymonde.

Her mother opens the door and is delighted to see me on her welcome mat. "Noor!"

Raymonde comes running into the hallway. "You're back!"

We hug and laugh, and they pull me into the living room. They look at me with slight concern – it must be obvious that I've been trekking all day. Before they can ask the questions I know are on their minds, I quickly explain my situation.

"Of course we'll help you," Madame Prenat says.

"You're a secret agent," Raymonde keeps repeating as they set me up in the living room to transmit my messages. We decide that it's much safer than the garden, as Nazis have taken over many of the neighbouring houses and the aerial could be spotted easily from top floor windows.

"Noor, dear," Madame Prenat says. "You have a good view of the front gate from that window. If you spot anyone, just run out of the back door. I'll hide your set."

I clasp Madame Prenat's hands. "Thank you."

She smiles at me. "What you are doing is very brave, and we must all help the Resistance however we can."

I get to work with my radio set as Raymonde watches from the sofa with interest. I'm so grateful that I've found a place to transmit from, as lives depend on it reaching London.

There are two agents who are being hunted by the Nazis after someone betrayed them by handing over their names and addresses. The poor agents only just escaped Paris by the skin of their teeth. They are currently hiding in a Frenchman's barn in the countryside, and I need to let London know to send the Lysander plane to pick them up. The agents will be ready and waiting tomorrow night at 2 a.m. to board the plane.

Later on, when we are drinking coffee in the kitchen, Raymonde asks me to explain what I do.

"Oh, I just help the Resistance out where and when I can," I say, wishing I could be a bit more honest with my old friend.

I withhold the details about how I most recently managed to organize the escape of thirty Allied airmen shot down in France.

Raymonde's house becomes one of my regular transmitting locations. I always make it a point to arrive by noon, complete my work and then spend the rest of the day relaxing. Raymonde and I often end up reminiscing about our days as children.

"Do you remember those story sessions you used to hold at Fazal Manzil?"

I nod and my mind wanders back to a distant time. My favourite was *The Monkey Chief*.

I am fourteen. Abba is no longer with us and Amma is still locked away in her room, grieving. It is Abba's brothers who now run the Sufi centre.

Fazal Manzil is still full of people who follow Abba's teachings of love, unity and peace. Many travel from other parts of Europe and bring their families. It is left to me to entertain the children when the adults meditate. I don't mind doing this; I love small children and it's an opportunity to practise my story-telling.

I've decided I'm going to be a children's writer one day. Some of my favourite stories are from the collection of Jataka Tales. These are ancient Indian tales full of self-sacrifice and doing what is right for the greater good.

"Gather around, children," I say in my most grown up voice. "Today, you will learn the tale of The Monkey Chief."

As the small group of children sit crosslegged on the floor, I notice my brothers sneak out of the room. I catch Khair's eye and she obediently sits, even as she stares wistfully at the door.

"Once upon a time, there was a monkey chief who lived deep in the heart of the Indian jungle. He was the tallest and bravest of all the monkeys. All would be well in monkey-world if it wasn't for the wicked human king. Can anyone guess why the king was so wicked?"

Six pairs of eyes stare at me in silence.

Khair's hand shoots up. *"The king wanted to eat monkey flesh."*

"Yes, very good. The king wanted to eat all the monkeys."

The children look suitably horrified.

"One day when the danger became too much, the Monkey Chief ordered his followers to leave that part of the jungle. Like all good leaders, he led the way. The monkeys jumped from tree to tree for miles and miles until they came to a big gap. 'We can't jump the distance between these two trees,' cried the monkeys.

'Don't worry,' the Monkey Chief declared. He laid his body between two branches of the trees to form a bridge. 'Jump over me, quickly!'

One by one, the monkeys all crossed the distance by jumping on the Monkey Chief's back. When they were all safely on the other side, the monkeys cheered and cried for him to get up. But the Monkey Chief could not get up because his back had been broken from the weight of all those monkeys.

He had sacrificed himself to save his followers. The king had been watching this from the riverbank with some amusement. But when he realized the Monkey Chief was hurt, he felt ashamed. He vowed to never kill monkeys for their flesh again."

"Noor," Raymonde's voice brings me back to the present. "What were you thinking so hard about?"

"Just about those story sessions."

"You were so lucky to get your stories published." She gets up to pick a book from the shelf. "Look, we still have our copy."

She hands me the book, worn and well-loved.

TWENTY JATAKA TALES

by

NOOR INAYAT KHAN

I hold the copy tightly to my chest. It is a solid reminder of another time, another world, before France was occupied by Nazis.

Chapter 17

Redhead

October 1943

The water in the bowl in front of me is stained blood red. I need to get rid of it before anyone notices. I stagger down the stairs to the back door of the building. Pushing it open, I take a quick peek and find the coast is clear. With one foot holding the door ajar, I lean out and empty the water in the gutter. It disappears, leaving only a slight red stain on the stones where the water has splashed. I dart back up the staircase and breathe a sigh of relief that I haven't bumped into any of my Nazi neighbours. On the occasions when I have done so, I've always greeted them with a large smile.

Back in my apartment, I keep my hair wrapped in the towel as it dries. This is the third time in a month that I've dyed my hair. Changing the colour of my hair has become a vital part of keeping the Nazis at bay. I've been a light brown shade, a blonde and now I'm trying something entirely new. I make sure to keep my hair tied up and under a hat when I leave the apartment so that the colour is not visible to my Nazi neighbours.

Standing in front of the mirror, I remove the towel and gasp. I was aiming for auburn but I've managed to dye my hair bright red. The colour clashes painfully with my skin tone. I pull a face. All I need now is a red nose and white face paint to look like a complete clown. I clutch a few strands between my fingers. The texture is like dry hay. Oh well, it's better to ruin my hair with dye than to be captured by Nazis. In an attempt to cheer myself up, I vow that once the war is over and I'm back in England, I will make an appointment at the poshest hair salon in London.

An hour later I leave my apartment for Raymonde's house in Suresnes with my hair tied under a summer hat.

"Jeanne-Marie."

It takes me a second before I realize that I am being called by my cover name. I turn with a bright smile to the Nazi officer leaning against the wall a few feet from my building.

"Hello," I greet him. "How are you?"

He shrugs. "Same as yesterday and the day before. We are just patrolling the streets."

"I must be on my way," I say apologetically. "I need to get to work."

"You are a children's nurse, yes?"

I nod a little too quickly and then try to compose myself so I don't look nervous to him, even though I am. It's not good that he remembers my name and occupation from when I told him the last time he stopped me on my way into my apartment building. He is showing way too much interest in me than is safe. I decide the best thing to do is get away before he asks me any probing questions about where I am headed.

Raising my hand in a little wave I take two steps backwards from him. "Bye then."

It is an effort to keep my jelly legs steady as I try to walk away as calmly as possible from the Nazi.

Chapter 18

The Beginning of the End

September 1943

I pull the scarf tightly around my neck. The café is freezing because the heating system is broken. The owner has apologized and offered me a free second cup of coffee. I insisted on paying, of course.

It does look a little odd that I'm the only customer, but I've arranged to meet Antelme's old contact, Gieules, here so have no choice but to wait. I've met him a couple of times already in passing, but this will be the first time we will be working together.

The café door creaks open and I raise my hand in greeting to the tall man. Gieules strides over to me.

"Why are you the only one in here?" he demands, making no effort to greet me first.

"It's empty because the heating isn't working," I explain,

craning my neck to meet his gaze. "And this was our arranged meeting spot."

He pulls a chair out, glancing over his shoulder before he sits. I notice how nervous he looks and think it's odd that, as a seasoned SOE agent, Gieules fails to mask his anxiety. Perhaps he has been working for the Resistance too long and is now paranoid. Does he see plain-clothes Nazis wherever he turns?

"London wants me to introduce you to some new agents," I say, getting down to business.

"Who are they? Have they been checked and re-checked?"

I shrug. "I don't know. I'm just following instructions from London."

He glances over his shoulder again. "Fine. Set up a meeting."

*

I walk as fast as I can to the apartment of a Paris businessman known only as Viennot. He is one of the few contacts that Antelme gave me.

"You can trust Viennot," Antelme had said. "He is a Frenchman doing his bit for the Resistance by employing agents as staff to give them cover stories."

143

I've got to know Viennot and trust him completely. It's why I'm rushing to him now as I have a very, very bad feeling about Gieules.

Viennot pulls open his door on my second knock and looks over my shoulder.

"Madeleine, what's so urgent? You're banging as if the Nazis are after you."

I pull a face. "Not funny."

He steps aside to let me in. "Coffee?"

"Yes, please."

I try to gather my thoughts as I watch Viennot fill the kettle with water. I have been in Paris for four months now and none of us have managed to get hold of decent coffee beans. We continue to suffer the awful stuff.

He places the kettle on the stove. "Now, what's wrong?"

"It's Gieules," I blurt out. "It's been over a week and I haven't heard from him." I frown, unsure if Viennot has even heard me over the whistling of the kettle. "Viennot?"

"I heard you, Madeleine."

I place my hands on my hips. "Well?" Viennot pours the hot water into the cups and the aroma of the coffee fills the room. Despite the awful taste that is to come, I find the smell soothing. Taking a deep breath, I lower my hands. "What if he's been arrested?"

Viennot hands me the cup. "So, contact him."

I want to roll my eyes. Does he think that the idea hasn't occurred to me? "I don't have his number. He always contacted me."

He takes a gulp of the piping hot liquid and then sets his cup down. "I have it somewhere. Wait." He disappears behind his desk and I can hear the rummaging and rustling of paper. "Here we go!" His head pops up and he hands me a scrap of paper. I dial the number and wait. The phone rings and rings.

"He's not picking up," I mouth.

Viennot says nothing, preferring to settle down in a chair with his coffee cup. I'm just about to hang up when it's answered.

"Hello?"

"Gieules," I cry with relief. "You're there!"

"Yes, Madeleine."

"Why haven't you called me?" I demand. "Is everything all right?"

"Yes, all fine." He hesitates, then, "We need to meet. There's a reason why I haven't called."

My heart sinks. "Are you all right? You haven't been ... you know."

"No, of course not," he replies quickly. "I'm still here, aren't I?"

"Well ... yes ... but—"

He doesn't let me finish. "Meet me tomorrow at ten o'clock at the Etoile."

"See you then."

I replace the handle and turn to Viennot. "He sounded a bit, I don't know ... detached."

"Detached?"

I nod. "You know, like he's not himself."

"You worry too much."

"It's my job," I answer a tad sharply.

Viennot throws his head back and laughs. "Yes, it is and you're very good at it. The Nazis must know of the single radio operator who has evaded capture for months."

*

The next morning Viennot and I make our way to the meeting point. He has insisted on accompanying me. Despite his relaxed demeanour I know he is worried about Gieules. A week's disappearance followed by an odd telephone manner has set us both on edge. We are a few blocks from the meeting point at the corner of Avenue Mac-Mahon and Rue de Tilsitt.

"Wait here," Viennot instructs, turning to me. "I'll go and

check that it's all clear. Gieules is expecting you, he won't know to look out for me."

I nod. Viennot is dressed in a black coat and hat. He could be any Parisian man walking by and much less conspicuous than a woman with my distinctive appearance. I watch him disappear from view and look around at the nearby shops, their windows empty of displays and their doors boarded up. The Nazi occupation has sucked the life out of Paris.

Suddenly, I hear urgent footsteps behind me and I spin around. Viennot is half running, half walking towards me. My heart sinks as I note his grim expression. He grabs my arm and sets a brisk walking pace. I don't have to ask him what's wrong – it's obvious. Gieules has betrayed me. He has betrayed all of us that are fighting the Nazi darkness. I don't ask for details, but Viennot provides them anyway. "He was there with six Nazi guards."

"Waiting for me?"

"Waiting for you."

"How could Gieules do this?" I blurt out.

"They got him," Viennot says grimly. "Maybe there was torture involved to give you up."

"I hope they didn't hurt him too much." Even after his betrayal, I can't help but be concerned.

Viennot gives me a funny look. "Forget him. Worry about

yourself. They know your codename and you now have a target on your head."

My legs suddenly feel weak and I stumble trying to keep up with Viennot.

"We need to disguise you," Viennot says. "Let's get your hair done and buy you some new clothes. You need to blend in as a fashionable Parisian."

A little laugh escapes me. I can't work out if it's because I find him funny, feel insulted at my supposed lack of Parisian chic, or because it's the only way to relieve some of the terror I feel.

October 1943

I catch my reflection in one of the few windows in Paris that is not boarded up. I am opposite the shop, leaning back into a doorway. My heart is racing and the sweat is trickling down my back. I am being chased by the soldiers. It seems all the officers have received orders to arrest a girl that looks like me. Small, slim and with a darker complexion than most Parisians. The makeover Viennot arranged for me has not worked. My professionally dyed hair and new clothes fail to disguise me from those who hunt me.

I strain to hear the sound of steel-capped boots on the cobbled streets. The sound of Nazis approaching becomes even harder to distinguish over the chatter of a group of small children, coming round the corner. What if the Gestapo are at the end of the avenue? They know to look for a girl by herself. I glance over at the children and their mother, now merely feet away. I suddenly remember my trick with the young mother and baby in Beaulieu during my field test.

With a deep breath, I step out into the street and fall in line with the group. The woman glances at me and her curious expression turns to one of fear. She doesn't like the fact that I am walking so close to them.

"I was just admiring your coat," I compliment.

Gosh, what a ridiculous thing to say. The woman gives me a funny look. She knows I am lying – her coat is threadbare. In another time it might have looked fashionable, but it has seen too many years of wear.

"Jean, come here," she snaps.

The little boy closest to me waddles over to her side. We are nearly at the end of the avenue now and I make an effort to remain calm. The woman says nothing. Does she suspect what I'm doing? Is she a resistance sympathizer or a Nazi collaborator? If she's the latter then all she needs to do is shout and point to me and Nazi officers will come running. In the end, I do not discover whose side she is on. A small alley comes into view and I disappear down it. Another turning and another and I manage to lose the Nazis. That was close.

I keep walking until I reach my meeting point with Viennot. I must look a right state because he stares at me, wide-eyed with concern.

"You're sweating, Madeleine."

I wipe my brow with the back of my hand.

"What's wrong?" he asks.

"Followed," I manage to say, trying to catch my breath. At this rate, I'm going to pass out before I speak a full sentence.

"By Nazi soldiers?" Viennot demands and then rolls his eyes. "Sorry, obvious question."

"This is the third time it's happened. Wherever I go, I can hear the click-clack of their boots. Never close enough to grab me, but always in the distance, approaching."

"You have to leave Paris," Viennot says. "It's too dangerous. I told you before that you are a target. Do you know that the Nazis offer a 100,000 franc reward for British agents that are caught? It would be incredibly tempting for a French person to betray you for that amount. You're lucky they haven't caught you yet."

"I can't leave, I'm the only radio operator," I blurt out.

"You'll be a dead radio operator if you don't listen. Go to the countryside; you'll be safe there until your return to London can be arranged."

Unexpected tears fill my eyes, caused by a combination of exhaustion, nerves and the feeling that I'll be failing in my duty if I flee to the countryside.

Viennot gives me a sympathetic look. "Madeleine, you have done your bit. We need a new anonymous radio operator now. It's not just your life you risk by remaining here. It's all of ours."

*

Normandy is lonely. After the bustle of Paris, even occupied Paris, I find the countryside rather depressing. I can't bear to be stuck in this farmhouse even though my hosts are wonderfully hospitable. The freshly baked baguette and cheese they give me for breakfast is the finest I've had in a long time. Yet, I cannot eat to my heart's content. It's as if I have a lump in my throat which makes swallowing hard. How can I enjoy food this good when millions are suffering under the Nazis?

I last exactly two days in Normandy before I head back to Paris. Viennot is not impressed when he sees me walk into his local café which is packed with Parisians. He sets his coffee cup down without saying a word, his displeasure clear to see.

"I can't stay away," I rush the words out to appease him. "It's not right. I feel useless and I want to do my part for the Resistance."

Viennot dismisses my loyalty with some anger. "The only thing you will succeed in doing here is getting the rest of us caught. Contact London and arrange your transport out of here."

The thought of returning home makes my heart heavy, but Viennot's tone is firm. Perhaps I am just putting my friends in danger by remaining here. "And one more thing, Madeleine," he continues. "Destroy your notebook full of codes. God help us if it falls into the wrong hands."

Though I'm shocked at Viennot's coldness, it is the push I need to convince me to return to London. I shove my hands deep into my pockets as I walk away. Does Viennot think I will betray my fellow agents if I am captured? I would never do that. Betrayal of those who trust you with their life is wrong. My great-great-great-grandfather was betrayed – I know I could never have betrayal on my conscience.

Chapter 19

Capture

October 1943

Before I make plans to leave France, I return to Suresnes one last time to say goodbye to my friends. As I walk through my childhood neighbourhood, I try to take it all in. Madame Prenat is tearful as I stand in her sitting room to tell her I am going back to England.

"I'm sorry to see you leave, Noor, dear. But you must absolutely flee if your life is in danger. When is your flight?"

"14th October," I reply. "Only two more days to go. I can't wait to see Amma and the family."

"Yes, your mother will be very happy to see you," Madame Prenat says. "She must have missed you greatly. You were always her rock after Inayat died."

I hug her tightly. "We will meet again when this war is over."

She steps aside so that I can say farewell to Raymonde.

"Thank you so much for everything." I say quietly.

"Of course," Raymonde smiles.

"I have something for you." Opening my hand, I place my gold compact in the centre of her palm. "This is to remind you of my heartfelt gratitude."

Raymonde's living room has been such a lifeline for my work that it is only right that this SOE gift is passed to her.

Raymonde hugs me. "Be safe, Noor."

"We will meet again," I promise. "The family and I will return to Fazal Manzil and all will be well."

*

My biggest mistake is returning to my flat. I should have known the Nazis would have my address. Having evaded some Gestapo officers on the streets, I turn the key with shaking hands, longing for the safety of the little room beyond. It's only when my racing heart slows to its regular beat that the smell of someone else's sweat hits my nostrils. A stranger is in my apartment.

A man steps out of the shadows. He is not in uniform but is wearing a suit. Who is he? I don't intend to find out. I turn to flee, but he crosses the distance and traps me against the door before I have a chance to open it. I struggle but he grabs my wrists and twists me around. The tiger in me is momentarily released as I bite into the flesh of his hands. He cries out as my sharp teeth break through the skin, before shouting in German and sending us both flying on to the sofa. His weight pins me down. I kick out, claw his face and push as hard I can, but his strength is too much for me to overcome. With a final effort, I jab him with my knee, and the Nazi rolls off me on to the floor. I can't believe my luck. I only need a second or two to dart to the door.

The cold steel of the gun's barrel against the back of my head ends that plan.

"Remain still or I will shoot," he growls.

I believe him. There is no reason why he wouldn't pull the trigger. With the gun still aimed at me, he reaches out to the telephone and dials with one hand.

"I have her," he says in broken German. "I need support." He then backs away from me to the corner of the room, the gun still on target.

I glare at him. I think I shocked him with my struggle – he must have expected me to be meek and submissive.

I remember Viennot's words about the 100,000 franc reward for capture of a British spy, and I am still furiously wondering who it is that has betrayed me when the Gestapo storm into the flat. They lower their guns and throw confused looks at the man who called for backup. I can see scorn in some of their eyes, as if to say "you couldn't handle her?"

"Well done, Pierre," says one in a mocking tone. "Always good to have French assistance."

So, it is a French collaborator who has captured me. I always thought it would be a German who would get the better of me.

"It's Monsieur Cartaud to you," the Frenchman snaps at the guard. "And don't let her fool you. She's vicious."

The soldiers don't look convinced and I give them no reason to change their minds. I leave with them quietly, flanked on either side.

Chapter 20

Interrogation

"We've been looking for you for a very long time."

I glare up at the man dressed in a stylish black suit. My hands are still tied from when the guards arrested me at the apartment.

"Madeleine," the man rolls the name on his tongue. "A French name. You do not look French – you have other blood it seems. Your colour is darker."

I know all about the Nazi obsession with the "master race". I've read about Hitler's speeches which are full of dangerous ideas that the German people are superior to everyone else. That they are the masters of all mankind. This man seems to be a fan of all that.

"Maybe I should begin by telling you my name," he says. "It is Ernest Vogt and it is my job to gain information from you. We can do it nicely, or we can torture you for the answers."

I feel a flash of fear, but I try to keep it off my face.

"Do you think that we did not know of Churchill's Special Operations Executive?" he says ever so slowly. "This game he plays with us to sabotage our efforts to bring peace to Europe."

I bite my lip to stop myself from scoffing. Do they call *this* peace?

"Mr Churchill thinks he is clever. He thinks he can beat our *Führer*." The pride is evident in his voice when he mentions Hitler. "The *Führer* has been sent by God to save us all and to let the German people take their rightful place as the leaders of the world."

I stare at him. How has he allowed himself to be fooled by such beliefs?

"Madeleine," he rolls my name on his tongue again. "Tell me who your fellow agents are."

I look at the floor, refusing to make eye contact.

"Give me names, Madeleine. Give me addresses."

He expects my silence. There is no impatience in his tone. He knows that his prisoners will not give up their secrets so easily. This is a dance and he is slowly taking the first steps towards me. It is only a matter of time before he grabs me and forces me to dance with him.

I will refuse though. I will not give up my secrets. I will not give up the names and addresses of my fellow agents.

I hold on to my resolution as I'm led from the holding room to a cell.

"I need to use the bathroom," I announce suddenly, an idea popping into my head.

"She speaks," Ernest says. He steps back and addresses two guards. "Take her."

The guards lead me to a small bathroom down the hall. I step inside and look around – just as I'd hoped, there is a window large enough for me to squeeze through. I turn to shut the door but a guard's foot blocks it.

"I'm not going to use the toilet with the door open!" I snap.

The guard glances at his colleague and then shrugs, removing his boot.

With the door now locked, I push open the glass and clamber out on to the ledge, careful not to look down. It's a big drop to the ground.

I take a deep breath. I just need to get off this building and go into hiding until I can make it to the Lysander to fly me back to England. I crawl along the ledge.

"Madeleine."

The voice startles me so much that I almost lose my

footing. Ernest Vogt's head is leaning out of a window further ahead.

"Don't be foolish. That's hard concrete below. If you drop, you die."

I glare at him. How did he know that I was going to attempt this? Maybe other prisoners have tried.

"Madeleine, think of your family. Amma all alone in London."

A small cry escapes me. How does he know about Amma?

"Take my hand now." He offers it to me and I consider the alternative. One small step off this ledge and I will go crashing down. Death would be inevitable. Amma would never see me again. I take his hand and allow him to pull me back inside. Then I break down and cry.

Later that day, I am lying on the bed in my cell, my head buried in the pillow when the door opens and Ernest Vogt walks in.

"I have brought someone to see you," he says.

I look up from my tear-stained pillow and gasp. Gilbert Norman, my childhood friend, is standing before me. He looks no different to the last time I saw him, just before the Prosper circuit fell.

Ernest Vogt turns to Gilbert. "Make her see sense," he snaps before exiting the cell.

"Hello, Madeleine." Gilbert's voice is low and flat, like he is somehow beaten.

"You've been here this whole time?"

He nods.

"You're working with them?" I ask, dreading the answer.

"No!" He denies before sighing in defeat and throwing his hands in the air. "Well, no and yes. The Nazis cannot be beaten. They have all of us under their control."

"Gilbert! No!"

"Please just tell them what they want to know."

"You mean you want me to betray my colleagues?" I almost shriek.

"It is over," he snaps. "Can't you see that?"

"For you, maybe. Perhaps even for me. But that doesn't mean we should betray those agents who are still trying to bring this darkness to an end."

"Madeleine—"

"Just go!" I turn my face away.

He leaves and I scowl at the wall. How could he do this? How could he help the Nazis? My mind flits to the traitors who caused my great-great-great-grandfather, Tipu Sultan's, downfall. How is this any different? Betrayal is betrayal.

The door opens again.

"Go away!" I scream, thinking Gilbert has returned.

"Come!" a guard commands. With no choice and with heavy limbs, I rise from the bed and follow him. I am led to Ernest Vogt's office which is warm from the fireplace. There are plush-looking chairs dotted around and a sofa against the wall. The shelves are filled with books. It seems he is going to interrogate me in more comfortable surroundings, luring me into a false sense of safety. I lift my chin, radiating defiance.

He smiles knowingly. "Some food, Madeleine."

I glance at the baguette, cheese and meat laid out on a side table. "No, thank you."

"Perhaps some English cigarettes and tea, then?"

I give in and accept.

"We have your notebook and the codes have already been deciphered."

I lower my face, burying my nose in my teacup. I realize now that I shouldn't have kept written copies of my transmission messages. But I was so sure from my training back in England that I was to keep a record. Did I misunderstand the instructions because that part of my training was so rushed? I suddenly remember Viennot's warnings to me to burn all my notes. God, he had been so right. If I'd done that, then these Nazis wouldn't have been able to get their hands all over that secret information.

He picks up some papers from his desk and hands them

to me. "These are copies of the letters you wrote to your Amma which were sent by Lysander flights."

I try not to show my shock. My letters were intercepted? Have we been infiltrated? Or is someone on our side betraying us?

"We also have the copies of your reports and messages to London, all neatly filed in your notebook." He pauses and uncurls his left hand which has been bunched in a fist, revealing four pills sitting in his palm. The pills that Maurice had given me as a precaution. I'd kept them tucked away in my suitcase. I'd never had the need to use them. I say nothing and Ernest opens a drawer to deposit them inside.

"I also know Maurice Buckmaster is the head of the French section of the SOE. We know all about Beaulieu in Hampshire. Should I go on?"

I say nothing.

"You did your parachute training in Ringway in Manchester."

I drop my head to hide the small smile. I never did parachute training so I know that he is bluffing. Perhaps he doesn't have my file after all. But the smile is wiped from my face when he shoves a pile of photos under my nose. I recognize the grounds of all of my training schools. Then the awful truth hits me – we must have been betrayed by someone in Britain. Only they would know about all of these locations. Why would someone who is safe and secure, far away from the danger here in France, sell out agents to the enemy?

I stare at him, aghast. "You have an agent in London?"

"We have agents everywhere. You may as well give up the rest. Your side will not win."

I have to ask the question that is burning me up. "How did you get hold of my letters to Amma?"

He hesitates and I think he is assessing whether to share this information with me. Finally, he says, "Do you remember the man who received you when your flight landed in France for the first time?"

"You mean Henri?"

He nods, his amused eyes revealing how much he is enjoying this. "Henri Déricourt is a double agent. He works for us. He makes copies of all letters that are carried on the Lysander."

I close my eyes at the thought of the betrayal.

"I told you before, Madeleine. We will win and you will lose. Save yourself by telling me what I need."

I snap my eyes open. "Never!"

He sighs and leans back. "How long can you keep this up? Look at your old friend Gilbert Norman. He is happily cooperating with us and coming to no harm."

"Gilbert is a traitor."

"But not you?"

"I would never betray my fellow agents!"

The scowl on Ernest Vogt's face is fleeting. So brief in fact that I would have missed it had my gaze not been fixed on him. He catches himself and smiles. It is nearly midnight when he sends me back to my cell.

*

Three days later, I have still told them nothing. To my surprise, Ernest Vogt has demonstrated remarkable patience but I know it is only a matter of time before they begin to torture me for answers. I am ready for it – braced for it. And I have vowed that I will not break. I will take the names of my colleagues to my grave if I have to.

Ernest Vogt walks into my cell and sits down on the hard bed beside me. "May I tell you about my friend Josef Goetz?"

I have no idea who he is talking about.

"Josef is a radio specialist. Once we capture the agent's radio sets – oh, and by the way, we have yours – Josef pretends to be the captured agent and radios back to London. As all the codes are in place, London doesn't suspect anything has changed. We demand arms, equipment and more agents, and London, gullible as they are, continues to send them. We even ask for the addresses of SOE agents and then break down their doors to arrest them."

I keep all emotion off my face although my heart is sinking further with every word. He pauses and I know what is coming next.

"We've already started to message London pretending to be you," he says, confirming my worst fears. "Mr Churchill's agents are falling into our trap. We'll know exactly who will be arriving on those Lysanders."

I bite my lip. I don't tell him that London will notice the messages aren't from me if my security checks are not included. It's the one code that I hadn't written down in my notebook. Ernest Vogt leans forward, close enough so that I can see that his eyes are not a pure blue, but speckled with green. His skin crinkles as he smiles again. "Now, we weren't sure if this was going to work. But we gave it a try anyway and it seems lady luck is on our side. London hasn't noticed that it's not you. They've been messaging back."

I can tell he is not lying. London would never respond if they thought I had been captured. I clench my jaw and glare defiantly. I will not allow this Nazi to see that he has affected me.

Ernest Vogt rises to his feet. "You've been most useful, Madeleine. Thank you."

That night I cry and cry. I can't help it. The Nazis have got the better of us. My fellow agents are in danger and there is nothing I can do about it.

Chapter 21

Escape

The loneliness is crippling. They've had me locked in here for weeks. Late one afternoon, I hear a noise and realize someone is being dragged into the cell next door. A new prisoner perhaps? Later, in the silence of the night, I try to make contact using Morse code – hoping they might understand it.

This is Madeleine. British agent. You?

The reply is immediate.

Leon Tage. British agent also.

I want to dance around my cell with relief.

Thinking of escaping. Want to try?

Yes.

Leon and I exchange messages every day. I'm careful not to give anything away in case he turns out to be a double agent placed next door to get information out of me.

A few days later another prisoner makes contact by slipping a note under my cell door. I realize the prisoner is taking advantage of the pen and paper that we are allowed to have. His message reads:

More notes under bathroom basin.

This new prisoner is called John Starr. All three of us continue to communicate through Morse code and notes, trying to figure out a means of escape. It is proving fruitless until, one day, a note from John reads:

Small window. Loosen frame with screwdriver

Has being kept locked up driven John mad? How are we to get hold of a screwdriver? But the note the next day reads:

Success! Have screwdriver.

It happens that John had offered to fix the cleaner's carpet sweeper, and after doing so, hid the screwdriver behind the basin. Genius! We take it in turns passing the screwdriver between us through the gap behind the sinks, trying to loosen the window frame. When it's my go I realize I can't reach the window. It's just too high. My bed is bolted into the wall and I can't move it. *What now?*

I climb on top of my mattress and see if I can lean over far enough to reach the window. Within seconds, I lose my balance and go crashing to the floor.

The cell door is flung open and two guards barge in.

"What are you doing?" one demands.

I sit up and cradle my right arm, which got crushed in the fall.

They both walk suspiciously around the cell but find nothing untoward.

They turn and leave.

I allow a few minutes to pass and then climb on the bed again. This time my balance is better. Slowly, slowly, over the next few days, I erode the plaster with the screwdriver, but I'm worried that the holes might be spotted if the cells are inspected.

It seems the same thought has occurred to John and his note reads:

The holes are visible. It will only take one sharp pair of eyes to notice them. They need to be covered.

I send my reply.

Leave it with me

The same day, I make a demand to one of the guards. "Tell Ernest Vogt that I need perfume and face powder."

A parcel arrives the same day. Even I am surprised at the fulfilment of my request. Perhaps Vogt thinks he can wear me down if he agrees to my wishes.

Even so, do the Nazis think me so vain that I need perfume and makeup as I sit alone in my cell? That same evening I crumble half the powder into two napkins and hide it under the basin with a note.

Use this powder to cover the holes

Finally, we are ready. On the night of our planned escape, we climb out of our windows, each carrying a bed sheet.

The cold air hits my lungs. It must be late November or December by now. No wonder it's freezing.

We scramble on to the roof and crawl across on our hands and feet so that we're not visible to those below. We manage to cross the distance to the next building in no time. Now, all we need to do is use our sheets as ropes to lower ourselves down. Nearly there. My heart is hammering.

Suddenly, the sounds of anti-aircraft guns shoot through the night. I stumble in shock and almost topple off the roof, but John reaches out to steady me just in time.

"What the—" Leon is looking up.

"It's an air raid," John cries. "'Just our luck!"

We flatten ourselves on to the roof and I feel as if my heart is going to explode. We're so close to escaping. But now our chances have been reduced to nearly zero. An air raid requires the Nazis to do a full check on all prisoners – I know this because there was an air raid only days earlier. They'll know we've escaped within minutes and the search will be on.

"We have to get off this roof now!" I say.

"Madeleine, no!" John objects.

Too late. I've already crawled to the edge and I tie the bed sheet to a pipe and swing down on to a window ledge. Praying that the room is empty, I kick the glass and climb into the room as the glass shatters. Seconds later, John and Leon swing in behind me.

We run down the stairs and through the doors on to the street. Too late. The Nazi soldiers are already waiting. They must have spotted us on the roof and swinging into the building. It would only take one pair of eyes to see our escape and to raise the alarm.

Breathing hard, I glare at the soldiers as they stand before me on either side with their guns. There is only the door behind us. I can hear John and Leon's ragged breathing in my ear. What to do now?

"Let's run back inside," I whisper.

"They'll shoot us," John says.

I glance back at the door trying to work out how my many steps will be required to reach it. At least five, I think. Will it be enough to outrun the bullets?

"Don't do it," John warns. "They'll shoot you."

Devastated that we came so close to escaping, my shoulders droop in defeat. Six soldiers march up, their steel-capped boots clinking on the cobbles. The next thing I know, I'm on the ground along with John and Leon, being punched and kicked and beaten. It's a miracle that I don't pass out from the beating.

Chapter 22

Imprisonment

November 1943

"Sign this letter," the man barks, "and you will be permitted to remain here at Avenue Foch."

I look up at him through swollen eyes. Some of those punches last night were directed at my face and my head is still throbbing with pain. He looks like a senior Nazi from his uniform.

"What does it say?" I mumble through teeth that ache and a swollen lip.

"You will promise not to escape again."

"I cannot sign that. It would be dishonest."

"Very well." He delivers my fate in an authoritative voice. "You will be transferred to Pforzheim Prison. You will become a 'Nacht und Nebel' prisoner. Do you know what that means?"

I keep my expression blank although dread starts to build

in my mind. I know enough German to understand.

"The full label is *Nacht und Nebel – Rückkehr Unerwünscht.*" His face takes on a look of glee. "Night and Fog – Return Not Required."

My fate is clear now. They are going to "disappear" me. I am going to be sent to their prison camps. I raise my chin in defiance, causing pain to shoot through my head. I will go to the camps with dignity – better that, than betray my friends.

*

I am immediately shoved into the back of a truck, driving out of my beloved city. There are no windows, so I cannot even take a last look at the sloping rooftops and grand streets of Paris. The journey seems to go on for ever and ever. Perhaps we drive for one night, perhaps two. There is no daylight in the truck and I am not let out when the driver stops for a break.

I fidget with the rope that binds my hands, needing to keep the blood flowing. I've suffered the worst pins and needles in my legs and arms and it's a marvel that I haven't collapsed from the blocked blood flow. I am soiled, hungry and cold, but I refuse to cry. I don't ever want the Nazi guards to see me look broken.

Finally, after what seems like a journey to the end of the world, the truck's doors are opened. The sudden daylight hurts my eyes and I squeeze them shut.

"Get up!" the guard orders.

I rub my eyes with my bound hands and slowly get to my feet. My legs feel numb but I force myself towards the doors, fearing that any delay on my part will lead to me being manhandled. I am nearly at the doors when the guard grabs my arm and hauls me out. It's a wonder that I don't break a leg as I hit the ground. A small whimper escapes me as the same guard yanks me up.

I take in my surroundings as I am dragged towards Pforzheim prison – a grey mass of concrete buildings to house Nazi prisoners. Row upon row of one storey rectangular blocks line the grounds.

I am shoved into an isolated cell with nothing but a filthy mattress and a bucket in the corner to serve as my toilet. The cell door slams and once again, I am left alone. The footsteps gradually disappear and then there is only silence. I sink to the hard floor, my tears unstoppable now.

The next morning my breakfast of runny gruel comes with the chains. My hands and feet are bound together with cold metal. I have to drag the chain around from one end of the cell to the other just to keep my blood flowing.

The worst part of all this is that they only allow me to be cleaned once a week. For seven days, I remain in the same clothes covered in sweat and dirt. Sometimes my skin and scalp itches, and my eyes feel sore from when I've rubbed them with filthy hands. At times like this, I would do anything to soak in a hot bath. No such luck though. The woman who cleans me uses a cold wet towel. As the days turn to weeks, I am grateful for this much at least.

The prison governor sometimes pops his head around my cell door and stares as if he can't quite believe that a young girl like me can pose such danger. I think he feels sorry for me and, after a month or so, he orders the chains to be removed. The freedom feels wonderful, but it doesn't last long. Though I don't cause any trouble, he orders the chains back on.

"My apologies," he says in a mildly regretful voice. "I do not deem it necessary to have you in shackles. If anything it costs me money to have a woman attend you."

"Then why?" I demand, trying to keep the tears at bay. I will not cry in front of this Nazi despite his sympathy for me.

"The order came from high above," he throws over his shoulder as he walks out.

The warden is the one who brings me food every day. I'm not spoiled for options here – it's either potato peel or cabbage soup on rotation.

A few months pass before I am permitted to step out of the cell. It's only for an exercise that lasts around forty-five minutes in the courtyard, every few days. Although I am heavily guarded and allowed no contact with the other prisoners, I cherish this time.

It is an effort but I try to keep the madness at bay by thinking of Amma and my siblings. I wonder how Vilayat is getting on with the navy, and whether Hidayat and the Resistance in the south of France are safe. I think of Khair, up in Edinburgh with her medical degree. I hope she's passing all her exams with flying colours and also makes time to visit Amma in Oxford.

I wonder if Amma still enjoys working in the hospital. Does she miss me? I wish I could write to her. What I wouldn't do for pen and paper right now! If only they would let me have these two things, the days would be slightly bearable. I could write down all that floats through my mind: the stories, the memories. A part of me has accepted that I will not be released so long as this war rages on.

*

I am tucking into the unsatisfying grub brought to my cell, when I notice there is a message scraped into the bottom of my metal bowl.

Three girls here.

At last! Contact with other prisoners. A message of reassurance. I look down at my fingernails. They are overgrown and sharp. It takes a while but I manage to scratch out my own message:

You are not alone. I am here.

The messages go back and forth but I find myself longing to meet these other prisoners. I want to make eye contact. Smile. Look into a human face that is not contorted with hatred.

*

I scratch the floor to add another sunrise. I have been keeping a tally of the days.

On American Independence Day, I scratched "Long Live 4th July" and on Bastille Day, 14th July, I scratched, "Long Live Free France".

Sometimes, I can't quite believe the number of little markings that have added up. I've been here nearly a year.

Two more months and it will be my anniversary. The thought makes me want to cry. Time ticks and still the Nazis carry on unleashing their cruelty.

My heart races every time I think about the war raging outside this prison. How many more people are dead? Who is winning? Has Britain been defeated? Has Churchill fallen?

Sometimes, I ask the female attendant when she comes for the weekly wash. Her cold blue eyes pierce through me. "The *Führer* is winning," is all she says.

I never know whether to believe her or not. Especially when I am woken by the thundering sound of fighter planes and bombers high up in the sky, before I hear the whooshing sound of bombs being dropped.

These planes must be British, sent across the ocean to attack some nearby German city. It's been five whole years of war, and still the bombs are falling on both sides. How much longer can the fighting possibly go on for? Abba's face comes into my mind and I remember his teaching on pacifism – he would be devastated at all the needless killing.

*

It is a chilly morning when the female attendant shoves loose, harsh fabric into my chained hands.

"Put this on," she says.

I unfold the rough fabric to reveal a makeshift dress. It looks like a sack.

"Why?" I ask.

"Because you're leaving."

My breath catches. I am leaving this prison?

"Where are you taking me?" I manage to unbutton the front of my dress despite the chains binding my hands together. I've done it so many times that it comes almost naturally.

"No questions," she snarls. "Hurry up."

I drop my dress to the floor and stand before her with my chin in the air, defiantly. I'm not sure whether I look serious or pitiful, now that I'm so malnourished. She scowls at me before unchaining my hands so that I can pull the sack-like dress over my head. Then the chains are back on and she leaves with my old clothes tucked under her arm.

I gulp down my gruel. It's tasteless as usual, but today I lick the bowl clean. I will need the energy. I wonder if I am the only prisoner leaving today and decide to leave a message on my bowl. It takes me a while to scratch out the words:

I am leaving

It is late afternoon by the time the guard comes to collect me. He pulls a key out of his pocket and bends down to unshackle me.

"Let's go."

I follow him out of the cell, and along the corridor, walking as if in a dream. As a cool, clean breeze blows against my face, for a moment I find it hard to care where I am going.

The guard leads me outside and stops beside a car. "Get in."

I climb in, surprising myself with my sluggish movements. My limbs have become stiff and I cannot move them easily. The car door slams and we begin to drive away from the prison, but the journey is not a long one. In just over an hour I am being led inside a brick building. I have no idea what this is. Perhaps another prison?

"What is this place?" I mumble.

To my surprise, he answers, "Karlsruhe Gestapo headquarters."

"Oh."

"In there." The guard points to a door. I walk on and see three women prisoners are already standing in line. I do a double-take as I recognize Yolande Beekman, the girl I met on the platform at Guildford station all that time ago. We had walked together to that beautiful Tudor mansion. When she looks in my direction, I nod my head in acknowledgment. She recognizes me and smiles. The other two women are strangers.

Another guard walks in with a clipboard and stands before us, commanding our attention.

"Yolande Beekman?"

"Eliane Plewman?"

"Madeleine Damerment?"

"Nora Baker?"

Each of us nods as our names are called.

I note that they are not using our cover names. The enemy knows everything about us.

Chapter 23

Dachau

We sit in silence in the car, huddled in the back. The Nazi in the passenger seat has his face turned towards us, a pistol in his hand. I have no doubt that he will use it if there is any sudden movement from any of us.

I am seated by the window and stare out at the fields. After being locked away for a year, the sight of the world makes me feel glad to be alive. The window is half open and the air blowing in feels wonderful. I'm reminded of the train journey from Delhi to Baroda, long ago, when I was thirteen and my family visited India after Abba's death. There was no glass in the window, only iron bars, and Vilayat and I had taken turns to sit beside it and feel the breeze. Tears come to my eyes as I think of my family and I brush them away quickly.

The drive does not last long. We are dropped off at a train station where another Nazi officer introduces himself to us, along with a guard holding a rifle.

"Hello, I am Max Wassmer," the man says in a tone that is almost friendly. "I will be joining your escort."

We stare at him, confused by his politeness. He is tall and imposing in his Nazi uniform and the gun on his belt is visible.

"It is going to be a long journey, ladies," he says. "I would rather we travel pleasantly together as companions, rather than as a guard with prisoners. If you will behave, I will behave."

"What do you expect from us?" Eliane demands.

He flashes a smile, revealing pearly white teeth. "Just don't try to run away."

We shrug. There is empty countryside all around us. We wouldn't be able to get very far without Wassmer's friend shooting us in the back. The train pulls into the station and we board it. From the corner of my eye, I notice Wassmer studying us. I wonder what he is thinking. His face is guarded, giving nothing away.

Yolande sits down next to me and takes my hand. "It's good to see you, Nora."

I link my fingers with hers. "You too."

The train delivers us to Stuttgart and we disembark, huddling together on the platform. There are a few people around us but no one pays us any attention. Perhaps the transfer of prisoners by armed guard on trains is normal now.

"We have an hour before our train to Munich arrives," Wassmer states. "You may talk amongst yourselves whilst I go and sit on that bench there. No funny business; my friend will not hesitate to shoot you."

We nod solemnly. At least we are free to talk.

"Where were you being held?" Yolande asks me.

I quickly give details of my capture and imprisonment. The girls nod grimly.

"I was dropped into France by the SOE to work with a network called Monk in Marseilles," Eliane reveals.

"Who was your leader?" I ask.

"Charles Skepper."

"Oh, I remember Charles," I say. "We flew in together on the Lysander plane in June 1943. That feels like such a long time ago."

"Doesn't it just," Yolande says.

"What happened to Charles?" I need to know the fate of the smiling, friendly man from that plane journey.

"The Monk network was infiltrated and Charles arrested," Eliane says gloomily. "Me and another agent called Arthur tried to rescue him but got caught ourselves. They hanged Arthur and I was held at Fresnes prison until now."

"I'm so sorry," I mumble.

Eliane nods, tears shining in her eyes. "And you girls?"

"I'm French," Madeleine says. "My father was the head postmaster in Lille. When France fell, I managed to escape to England with the help of the Resistance. The SOE trained me and I returned to sabotage the Nazis, but I got caught up in a Nazi raid within days of landing. I didn't even get a chance to deflate the tyres of a German car."

We smile at her joke, although it is more sad than funny.

"Were you at Fresnes as well?" Eliane asks.

Madeleine nods. "First at Avenue Foch and then at Fresnes."

This leaves the story of Yolande. We turn to her.

"I was the radio operator for the Musician circuit in northern France. Our missions were going really well." We instinctively lean in together, eager for details. "The Nazis transported their arms and troops through the canal in north-east France. We managed to destroy the lock gates that control the water flow in the canal."

"Hurray!" We cheer together.

"We were on a roll but the Nazis were determined to track us down. One day, I was just sitting in a café with my colleague when the Gestapo appeared out of nowhere and arrested us. I was hauled to Avenue Foch, then Fresnes."

These are our stories: trained by the SOE, flown in to sabotage and subvert, captured and then imprisoned.

"Any idea where we're headed?" I ask. "What's in Munich?"

"I asked Wassmer on the train," Madeleine says. "He says we are being taken to a farming camp. They are going to make us work for our supper."

"I'd prefer that to being locked up all day," I say. The thought of being allowed to be with other prisoners will be a relief. Who would have thought eye contact and a smile could mean so much?

"Ladies!" Wassmer booms. "The train is pulling in. Stick together."

He finds us seats by the window and the German countryside speeds past, exhibiting exceptional beauty with every passing mile.

"Look at those." Madeleine points to the mountains in the distance. "So majestic."

"Those are the Swabian Mountains," Wassmer says with a hint of pride in his voice. "Germany is a land full of beauty."

"Pity about the people in charge," Eliane says under her breath.

I nudge her, warning her to be quiet. Wassmer gets to his

feet and looms over Eliane. I close my eyes, expecting him to strike her.

"Thank you," Eliane says.

I snap my eyes open. Why is Eliane thanking the Nazi? I cannot believe what I am seeing – Wassmer is holding out a packet of English cigarettes. Eliane takes one and passes the rest around. I pick one out and Wassmer lights it for me.

"Enjoy," Wassmer says before walking away. I stare after him. This whole situation feels too good to be true, and I can't help the sense of foreboding. Why is this Nazi officer being so nice?

Yolande's eyes are on Wassmer. He has taken a seat further up the carriage and is engrossed in his notebook. Perhaps he has moved away because he wants peace and quiet. Of course there is no chance of escape. The armed guard is sitting but a few feet away.

"Let's talk in English because he doesn't understand," Yolande says, jerking a thumb at the guard.

With Wassmer out of earshot, this is my chance to ask for news. The hum of the train also makes it easier not to be overheard.

"Have you heard anything about the war?" I whisper.

Yolande nods. "I've heard from the new prisoners at Fresnes that the Nazis are losing. Paris has been liberated."

"Oh!" My hand is over my mouth. I cannot believe it. My Paris is free. At last! This is the best news. "What else?" I ask urgently.

"D-Day was a success," Yolande provides.

I frown slightly. "What's that?" I ask.

"On 6th June 1944, the Americans and the British Empire forces landed on five beaches along the coast of Normandy."

The frown eases off my face and my eyes widen with awe. "How many?"

"They say more than 150,000 troops."

My hand is over my mouth again to stifle the whoop of joy.

Yolande grins at me. "We're taking the world back."

"Are you sure? What if the prisoners you met are lying?"

"Why would they lie? They are the same as us. Also, have you looked at the senior Nazis' faces closely? They look worried."

We all glance at Wassmer. He is buried deep in his notebook.

"Have we really turned a corner?" I ask, barely able to believe it. "The end is in sight?"

Yolande nods happily. "Indeed. We just have to wait to be liberated from these thugs by our approaching troops. Not long now hopefully."

I nod.

Not long now.

Liberté.

*

Wassmer walks back to us just as the train chugs into Munich station.

"One more change," he says.

We board another train and settle down. Wassmer looks between us and I wonder if he is noticing the change in our spirits. We all feel lifted after our conversation about the success of the Allied troops.

"Where is this train taking us?" Eliane asks.

"Dachau," Wassmer replies.

I've heard about Dachau before. Racking my brains, I remember what we learned about it during training at Beaulieu. It was the first concentration camp that Hitler built, near his base in Munich. Why did Wassmer tell Madeleine earlier that we were being transported to a farming camp where we would work?

I give my head a little shake to ward off the anxiety. The Allied troops are on their way. That is all I need to focus on – people are coming to rescue us soon.

It is approaching midnight when the train pulls into Dachau station. No vehicle awaits us as the camp is within walking distance. We trudge silently between Wassmer and the armed guard.

"Hurry, ladies," Wassmer commands. "I need to deliver you and be on my way."

"What does that say?" Madeleine whispers as we approach the gates.

I don't know what she's talking about. "What am I looking at?"

"There, in the middle of it."

I follow her eyeline and see it.

ARBEIT MACHT FREI

"Work will set you free," I translate and a sense of foreboding returns. We walk through the gates and further into the compound. This is another camp of mass concrete. Rows and rows of single storey buildings to house the prisoners.

Though I've heard about the camps, nothing prepares me for the reality.

A gasp escapes me when my gaze falls on a group of women and children standing in a line outside a building with a chimney that is blowing out a thick cloud of smoke.

They are being herded by soldiers so that none can sneak off. It is not that they are out so late in the night that horrifies me, but their appearance. Every woman's hair has been shaved off. There is not a single strand of hair between all of them. Even the small children that clutch their mother's skirts have shaved heads. And all of them are dressed in blue and white striped dresses.

The poor children in striped pyjamas are making my heart hurt. They do not deserve this. Nobody does. I avert my gaze to the faces of the adults and see a mixture of expressions; fear, bewilderment, despair and defeat. But in some I also see defiance. Perhaps this is the end, yet these people won't go into the night with their heads bowed.

I raise my chin. I want to be one of these people; defiant in the face of darkness.

Chapter 24

Liberté

September 1944

The guard steps forward and drags me from the other girls. They try to protest but are only shoved to the ground for their efforts. I try to remain calm as I am pushed into a building and then into a very small cell. I try to breathe hard. I survived months and months in chains. What can this guard do to me now? It turns out that he can do a lot. In the next few minutes I feel as if my body is about to break from the beating he unleashes on me.

"You cannot be permitted to live," he says softly, his voice a contrast to his brute force. "You are a British spy and you know too much."

"I don't know anything," I mumble, desperate for some water.

He doesn't press the point. Instead he says, "The order has come from Berlin by Herr Himmler himself."

I know that name. He is one of Hitler's right-hand men and the architect of the concentration camps. He is the one who has granted total power to the police and soldiers to kill anyone whose beliefs are different to the Nazis. I know enough about him from my training that just his name inspires fear. "What order?"

"That the British agents cannot be allowed to survive in the event of the war being lost."

Yolande's prisoner friends were correct; D-Day was a success. "You are losing the war?"

My answer is a kick in the ribs.

"Your three friends are already dead."

I close my eyes, my heart aching for Yolande, Eliane and Madeleine. Earlier on the train we'd vowed that no matter what torture the Nazis had planned for us, we would survive the camp until it was liberated. And now my friends are dead and their three families will never see them again.

Why have the Nazis kept me alive?

Another guard enters the cell. He is holding something in his right hand. It gleams in the light and I narrow my eyes, squinting to see what it is. And then it hits me – it is water. The guard is holding a glass of water. I drop my eyes. I don't want to seem desperate for it … even though I am. They will use it against me. They will let me have one sip, promising me paradise, and then snatch it away.

The guard places it on the floor. I try to ignore the glass, but it's so hard. The water calls to me. It promises to slip down my throat and awaken the parts of me that are dying, but I am afraid that if I reach out he will kick the glass. They've been torturing me for hours. Why would they show me mercy now?

"Drink," the soldier says.

I obey and reach out to the water but his boot tips it before my fingers can brush the glass. The water splashes on to the dirty floor and for a moment I contemplate licking it. Perhaps I could save a few drops on my tongue.

I don't come close to the spilt water. The steel-capped boots have me curling into a ball in the other direction.

Much later that same night my fingers touch my face. The skin feels caked, as if I'd plunged my head into a bucket of mud and allowed it to congeal. But I know it isn't mud. It's blood. Blood that has oozed from my nose, ears and mouth as the boots connected with my soft flesh. The blows to my head are kinder than the ones to my ribs and stomach. When the steel-capped toes strike against my skull, darkness envelopes me into its fold for a time. It's a relief.

I hear them talking about me. "She looks like a doll. She should have broken by now."

I wonder why I have not broken. How am I still alive? That final kick should have surely punctured my heart.

"*Babuli.*"

It's Abba's voice. How can that be?

"*Babuli.*"

There it is again. Despite the pain, I look up. I blink once and then again. Abba is standing there. I rub my eyes with hands that are suddenly clean of blood.

"*Babuli,*" Abba says for a third time.

"Abba," I whisper.

"Yes, my *jaan,*" he says. *Jaan* means life. He has called me his life.

I feel strange. I close my eyes expecting Abba's mirage to disappear when I reopen them, but he is still here.

"Let's talk," he says, as the tears fall from my eyes. "Why are you crying, *Babuli*?" He sits down on the ground so that he can stroke my hair.

"Because I've let everyone down in the SOE, and Amma must be so worried about me. I shouldn't have allowed myself to be captured. It was so silly of me to return to Paris in those last couple of days."

"You did your duty."

"And got caught," I say bitterly.

"Many, many people have been caught and lost their lives for this fight. You are not alone in this fate. Do you regret it?"

"No," I protest. "I joined for a good reason. I wanted to help end this war."

"Yes, you did. You joined for the right reasons. You chose light and humanity. Those that sit by and do nothing are complicit."

I wipe my tears. "You have shown exceptional courage and dignity," Abba says gently. "You have not lied nor have you betrayed your friends and colleagues. You have taken everything that the Nazis have done to you."

"It hurts, Abba. My whole body hurts."

"I know, *Babuli*." He looks increasingly sad. "I wish more than anything that I could take away the pain. Alas, I cannot – it is yours to bear."

"You are right, Abba. I remained true to your teachings. I did not lie and neither did I betray my friends."

"I am so proud of you."

I bask in his pride and then the sadness returns. "I will never marry nor have children."

"No, you will not. But your name will live on. The world will remember Noor-un-Nissa Inayat Khan, writer and Churchill's courageous spy, long into the future.

They will mark your bravery and sacrifice when this war is a distant memory."

"You think so?"

"You will be remembered, Noor. Sacrifice is never forgotten."

The door creaks behind me. The soldier has returned.

"Abba, don't go," I croak. "He can't see you."

It's too late. Abba is gone and my gaze falls to my hands. The dried blood has returned.

And so, this is my story.

It ends here in this prison cell of Dachau concentration camp. It is not easy to defeat a tiger. A tiger has to be betrayed.

I feel sad that I will not live to see the end of this darkness that has invaded the earth. But I have contributed to the emerging light. The light will come. It must.

"Get up."

I try to do the guard's bidding in order to avoid the boot.

"Kneel."

He has no patience. He jerks me up by my hair. I know what it coming. Yet, I feel calm. I did what was right.

The cold metal scrapes the back of my head.

I barely summon the energy for my last words.

"*Liberté.*"

Freedom.

AUTHOR'S NOTE

I would like to begin by saying how incredibly honoured I am to bring Noor-un-Nissa Inayat Khan's story to the attention of young readers. Noor's story has held a fascination for me from the moment I heard about a brave British-Indian woman who was Winston Churchill's spy in the Second World War.

Researching Noor, I discovered that there were many sides to the girl who was born in Russia, raised in France, trained for war in England and executed in Germany. She was a princess belonging to an Indian royal family that was overthrown and exiled from their home and a daughter raised by a pacifist father who taught her about the principles of truth, loyalty and sacrifice. She was proud of her Indian ancestry, unafraid to publicly support the vision of a free and independent India when the country was still under British rule and the woman brave enough to position herself at the forefront of the war against the Nazis. And she was a brilliant children's author.

Noor's gentle manner and appearance created doubt in the minds of some of her senior SOE officers. They didn't think she would have the steel to see her mission through, and would betray the rest of her colleagues by breaking under torture.

Noor proved them wrong.

She did not flee back to London at the first sign of danger. She chose to remain at her post as a radio operator, the vital link between Nazi-occupied Paris and London. More importantly, the war records show that even after being captured, Noor did not reveal the names of her colleagues to the Nazi officers. She refused to betray them even as she suffered extreme torture. Her loyalty, no doubt, saved the lives of countless SOE agents.

In short, Noor was a heroine.

Her life was brief, but her passion to confront the evil of fascism and her ultimate sacrifice grants her a place in our history books.

As a girls' rights activist, my school workshops focus on how to campaign for girls' rights using the democratic process of our country. Pupils learn how to design petitions, how to write a letter to their MP and how to organize a social media campaign on an issue of their choice. We also study how women from our history, such as Noor, contributed to the positive change that we all benefit from today.

Noor was of white-American and Indian descent, and a Muslim. But she cannot be claimed by any one race or faith. Her sacrifice was made so that ALL people could be free of fascism. Her life and death contributed to the liberty we all enjoy in Great Britain, in Europe and around the world. We are free because of the courage shown by Noor and we should remember and honour her, along with the millions of soldiers, airmen, and sailors, and the women from the Women's Auxiliary Air Force (WAAF) and First Aid Nursing Yeomanry (FANY) who did so much to defeat the Nazis.

And we must do all we can to stop it happening again.

I would like to thank those who contributed to the development of this book. Firstly, my agent, Sophie Gorell Barnes of the MBA Literary Agency. Thank you, Sophie, for backing the idea from the very start and making it happen. To Emily Hibbs for the invaluable feedback on the early draft and to my editor, Nazima Abdillahi, for supporting Noor's story with all its sides. You helped me tell it exactly as I wanted it to be told.

Sufiya Ahmed

IMPORTANT DATES

November 1940

Noor joins the Women's Auxiliary Air Force (WAAF).

June 1943

Noor is given the codename "Madeleine" and joins the "Prosper" Resistance network in Paris, becoming the first female radio operator to be sent into Nazi-occupied France.

October 1943

Noor is betrayed and arrested by the Gestapo. Within minutes of her arrival at the Gestapo headquarters, she attempts to flee from a bathroom window but is caught.

November 1943

Noor is transported to Pforzheim prison in Germany where she is held in solitary confinement and tortured. Despite this, she does not betray any of her fellow agents.

12th September 1944

Noor is sent to Dachau concentration camp. A day later, she is executed along with three other female SOE agents. Her body is cremated at the camp.

29th April 1945

Dachau concentration camp is liberated by the Allied forces, seven months after Noor's execution.

16th January 1946

Noor is posthumously awarded the Croix de Guerre with Gold Star (the highest French civilian honour). Noor is known as Madeleine of the Resistance and "Cours Madeleine", a square in Suresnes is named after her.

14th August 1947

British India gains its independence from the British Empire and splits into two new countries; India and east and west Pakistan. East Pakistan later splits to become Bangladesh in 1971.

April 1949

Noor is posthumously awarded the George Cross, the second highest award of the United Kingdom "for acts of the greatest heroism or for most conspicuous courage in circumstance of extreme danger". Only 408 people have ever been given this award, 394 of them men.

NOOR-UN-NISSA INAYAT KHAN'S LEGACY

Over the years, Noor has been granted several honours in recognition of her efforts and sacrifice. Here are just some of the ways her legacy has been recognized and memorialized.

To honour Noor, a statue stands in Gordon Square, London where she lived with her abba and amma as a baby.

Noor's name is inscribed on plaques at: Dachau crematorium, Germany; Dachau Remembrance Hall, Germany; Fazal Manzil, France; St Paul's Church, Knightsbridge, England; RAF Memorial in Surrey, England.

Noor is honoured with a blue plaque at 4 Taviton Street, near Gordon Square. The blue plaque scheme honours notable people who lived or worked in that building. Her name is also inscribed on the Commonwealth Memorial Gates near Hyde Park, London.

SOLDIERS OF THE BRITISH EMPIRE

At the start of the war in 1939, Britain possessed an empire that covered a quarter of the globe and ruled 24 per cent of the Earth's population.

The British government called on its subjects from as far away as India, Canada, Australia, New Zealand, South Africa,

Zimbabwe, the West Indies and other colonies to join the fight against Hitler.

Five million soldiers enlisted, of which 2.5 million came from India alone. The British Indian army was the largest volunteer army in history.

After the war, 4,000 were decorated with military awards and 17 members of the British Indian Army were awarded the Victoria Cross, the highest and most prestigious award of the British honours system.

Additionally, the Indian Independence movement that Noor was so passionate about concluded three years after her death.

THE FATE OF NOOR'S COLLEAGUES

Like Noor, many of her colleagues mentioned in this book were real people and faced a similar fate to Noor at the hand of the Nazis. Sadly, Gilbert Norman, France Antelme, Henri Garry, Madeleine Damerment, Yolande Beekman, Diana Rowden, Eliane Plewman and Leon Faye were all executed by the Nazis.

Cecily Lefort died in a German concentration camp. Henri Déricourt, John Starr, Professor Balachowsky, Robert Gieules, Viennot and Marguerite Garry all survived the war.

DISCUSSION QUESTIONS

a) Noor's father was a pacifist who did not believe in violence or war. Why do you think she and her brothers broke away from this principle to join the war efforts?

b) Who was Gandhi and what was his vision?

c) What did Noor and her great-great-great-grandfather Tipu Sultan have in common?

d) Adults always talk about the world wars and why it shouldn't be allowed to happen again. How do you think it can be prevented from happening again?